The Christmas Contest

The Christmas Contest

Scarlet Wilson

TULE
PUBLISHING

Chapter One

W ELL HI FOLKS *and welcome to KNWZ, and guess what? It's getting to be that time again. You know? Christmas time! We love Christmas time at KNWZ and we've got something very special this year to help you all celebrate the season of goodwill. Find your favorite Secret Santa, your most intelligent Mrs. Claus, your brightest Christmas fairy, or your most Christmas-crazy work colleague, because...you're going to need them! This year we're hosting a special Christmas quiz, the winner of which will win ten thousand dollars for the charitable organization of their choice, just in time for Christmas! So, roll out your Christmas cracker. Register online to take part in our first stage Christmas quiz. But don't be fooled, it's not for the faint of heart. Our online quiz will sort out the Grinches from the True Elves and will leave us with ten quarterfinalists. After that, live on air, we'll host our own quiz to find our two semifinalists. They'll be in a fortnight-long battle with seasonal challenges to find our biggest Christmas know-it-all. Someone will win ten thousand dollars for their favorite organization. Could it be you? Register now and spread some of the Christmas love and may the best Christmas nut win!*

The radio announcer cut to the latest version of *Jingle-*

Bell Rock as Lara Cottridge came back through to the office with a plate of Christmas cookies. They were her brand-new recipe, perfected in the early hours of this morning. She slid them onto the desk as her colleagues gathered around, hands swiping cookies as they spoke.

"That's got to be you."

"You're the biggest Christmas nut we know."

"Does anyone know as many useless Christmas facts as you?"

"They're not useless." Lara took a swipe at the hand whose owner had flung the last insult before she picked up a cookie for herself. "Hmm," she said, nibbling at the edge. "Maybe a little more nutmeg?"

She settled in her chair. "What do you all think?"

Her five coworkers leaned on the edge of her cubicle. "We think you should enter that contest," Abby said.

Lara frowned. "What contest?"

Rae made a strangulated sound. "The one that is built entirely for you."

Lara looked at the faces staring at her. She held up the cookie again. "Cinnamon?" she queried.

All five let out a collective sigh. "Lara!"

"What?" She laughed now. "I have no idea what any of you are talking about."

Abby shook her head, pulling up a chair alongside her. "Didn't you listen? The announcer was practically crying out your name."

2

Lara frowned. "What can I say? I was distracted. Have any of you looked outside?" She stood up and pulled back the window blinds to open them. Briarhill Falls was covered in another thick layer of snow. From the admin office in the hospital, they had a clear view of the main street in Briarhill Falls. The array of shops with multicolored awnings, now coated in snow; the three-tiered frozen water fountain in the town square; waves of mist hanging over the Christmas tree lot at the far end of the street with a few green treetops floating above the surface, giving them the illusion of hovering in midair. Just one look was enough to send tingles across Lara's skin. The people wrapped up in their best winter wear—splashes of bright red, blue, and green against the white snow—bustled about their business. If she could breathe in the outside air from here, she swore she could smell fresh fir scent mixed with gingerbread, berries, and cinnamon. She smiled at the cookie in her hand.

Abby rolled her eyes. "What? More snow." Slapping her hand to her chest, she collapsed into her nearby chair. "Well, strike me down—it's Vermont. In winter. What a surprise."

Rae tugged at the sleeve of Lara's red shirt. "Didn't you say your grandmother's retirement home needs their gardens redone?"

Lara sat a little straighter. "Well, yeah. The last guy bailed on his contract. He even took all the money with him—probably to Hawaii—and they haven't had the funds to take on someone new."

It was almost like the rest of the women realized this was the best way to rope Lara in. "Wouldn't you like it if your grandmother's retirement home could have the giant tree in its courtyard like it normally does?" Rae asked.

Lara frowned. "Of course I would." She sat the cookie down, "What are you all talking about?"

Rae slipped her arm through Lara's. "It seems your little goldmine brain full of useless Christmas facts could actually come in handy. Our favorite radio station just announced they'll be offering ten thousand dollars for whomever wins their Christmas quiz. All you have to do is register online."

Lara pulled back a little. "Ten thousand for winning a Christmas quiz?" That was a *lot* of money.

Abby nodded. "Yeah. It was just on the radio. Register online, answer the preliminary questions, then do a few other things. All to win ten grand, which will be awarded to your favorite organization."

"You'll ace it," Rae said quickly. "No one knows Christmas like you do."

"This sounds too good to be true. It can't be that simple."

Abby gestured toward the radio. "KNWZ says it is. Why don't you apply at lunchtime?"

Lara swallowed, wishing she'd made coffee to go along with the cookies. Ten thousand dollars? Her grandmother's place could really do with the money. Ever since the contractor had run off with the gardening fund, the outside of the facility had become a little neglected. When the residents had been informed there was no budget for decorating the central courtyard this year, she'd sensed the despondency in the air. The courtyard usually displayed a giant real Christmas fir, decorated in whatever shades the residents had picked that year. The thought of it not being there had made Lara's stomach sink. And it wasn't just the residents who were sad about it—the staff were, too. The outdoor space played such a large part in the holiday celebration. A candlelight Christmas service had been held in the courtyard every year since her grandmother had moved in. This year, the plans had understandably changed.

"I'll think about it," she said as she turned back to her computer.

How hard could a Christmas contest be? For as long as Lara could remember, she'd adored everything about Christmas. Useless Christmas facts were her one vice.

But she didn't want to do the contest in full view of everyone in the office. Nerves might get the better of her. Tonight. She'd do it when she got home. Closing her eyes for a second, she pictured the faces of the residents if they could get their beloved Christmas fir this year. Excitement already buzzed through Lara. This might even be fun!

THE RADIO PLAYED in the background as the kids practiced.

"Hey, Mr. Winter. How about you do that?"

Ben looked up from where he was helping some of the younger kids shoot baskets. The gym hall was packed. When he volunteered, he always managed to have a good turnout for the afterschool program. It helped he was an ex-baseball player. He'd been picked up by one the major league teams while in college, but then crashed out due to injury before quite hitting the big time. So near, yet so far.

This time of year, there was no baseball in Vermont. He'd spent the last few years volunteering and coaching all sports here after school. He'd coached football, netball, hockey, basketball, and, of course, some baseball. Just enough that it didn't make his old injury ache too much. He believed there was a sport out there for every kid. And he was happy to help them find something they loved.

Last year, he'd taken a group of kids orienteering. Others had attended a rock-climbing facility. He'd helped some of the senior girls set up spin classes. Even the kids who decided they'd hated all sports would join in for a game of dodgeball. He'd even made some inquiries about a yoga instructor teaching a class in the program. Anything to help the kids increase their endorphins and their feel-good factor.

"Hey, Mr. Winter!"

Ben looked up just in time to see a basketball flying at him. He jumped up and caught it, landing with a thud on the floor. The shockwave reverberated through him, and he glanced down. The gymnasium floor badly needed to be replaced. Partly due to him, this place was used constantly. Parts of the floor were worn, patchy in places, with cracks starting to appear. At some point, a health and safety assessment would likely say it couldn't be used anymore and the school district definitely wasn't getting rich soon, which meant no budget for a new floor.

He tuned to what the kids had just said, strode over to the office and listened to the announcer on the radio.

Ten thousand dollars just to answer questions about Christmas? It was the family joke that there wasn't a thing about Christmas that Ben didn't know. Some people collected baseball cards or lunch boxes. As a kid, Ben had collected weird and wonderful Christmas facts. It had helped him on many a trivia night in one of the local neighborhood bars. But now? If he closed his eyes right now, he could imagine this place with a brand-new, sprung floor that would work wonders for the basketball matches and gymnastics taking place in the school. Would a school be considered an organization worthy of the prize? One phone call would let him know.

Several of the kids crowded into the office with him.

"What do you think, Mr. Winters?"

"Could you do it?"

"You can name all the reindeers in under ten seconds!"

He laughed. It was true. "I'm not sure that's a skill, Cody."

"Sure it is!"

He shuffled some papers on the desk, as he was watched by what seemed like a dozen sets of hopeful eyes. He held up one hand. "Let me think about it, guys. I'll let you know."

Shooing them out of the office, he followed and started a new game of dodgeball. But his brain was in another place. He'd been here as a volunteer coach for the last five years—after his baseball career had bombed because of his injury. He'd left Los Angeles to return home to Briarhill Falls, bought his woodshop, and after some persuasion from a local kid, had decided to drop in at his old high school to see if he could help in any way. They'd welcomed him with open arms.

As he watched the kids laughing and playing, he felt his heart swell. He could do this. He could. He'd win them a brand-new gym floor for Christmas.

Chapter Two

L ARA SETTLED DOWN in front of her computer, a small bowl next to her with some popcorn and a glass with wine. She was ready to do this, but her stomach was churning. Not quite sure why she was nervous.

It was only a silly contest.

She kept telling herself that as she registered online on the radio station's website.

But as soon as she'd confirmed her email address, red letters flashed on the screen in front of her.

KNWZ wants to announce that we've had the highest registration in our station's history for our new Christmas contest! As a result of this, it's likely that we'll stop registration in the next few days to stop our website from crashing! Good luck, folks!

Lara's stomach gave an uncomfortable squeeze. Okay. It was now or never. If she wanted a chance of winning, she couldn't delay.

She looked at the large green *start* button on the contest page. Her fingers hovered for a second, and then she finally pressed it.

BEN WAS TIRED. After the school session, he'd gone back to his workshop to put in a few more hours on a set of chairs he was making for client. He took pride in his work. The hand-made wooden table and chairs had taken the better part of a month, and they still weren't quite finished. He wouldn't let the order leave his workshop until he was sure every piece of wood was as smooth as silk.

He stretched out his back before collapsing onto the sofa. After flicking on the TV, Ben rolled his shoulders a few times, trying to relieve some of the aches and pains, still thinking about what the kids had said today. After they'd mentioned the contest, it was like every step he took on the gymnasium floor reminded him how much it needed to be replaced. Every basket scored had reinforced just how important this space was to the kids. The camaraderie, the belonging, the teamwork—it was important, especially for the kids who'd previously struggled.

Ben's style had gelled with the kids. He knew that some of them still had a bit of hero worship going on over him, but he was always honest with them. He'd tried his best to get in the pros, got injured, and had to make a new plan. Life sometimes got in the way of dreams. And it allowed him to constantly reinforce the message—*life isn't about what happens to you, it's about how you react to what happens that matters.* Briarhill Falls had faced a few challenges of its own.

Factories had closed. Businesses struggled. His own wood-shop just managed to tick over into the green. Often, he did jobs for lower prices than he should, just to help others out. But working with his hands made him happy…and coaching at the school allowed him to keep his love of sports alive.

He pulled his laptop over to him and flicked it open. It only took a few moments to find the radio station's website and the contest link. After he registered, he didn't hesitate when the green button appeared.

Start.

IT TOOK A few seconds for Lara to register what had just happened. A large timer had appeared on the top corner of the screen. A red balloon flashed up.

Answer as many questions as you can in two minutes.

Panic washed over her. She hadn't been expecting this. The questions were simple enough. Too simple even.

Where was Jesus born? What gifts did the Wise Men bring? Name all of Santa's reindeers. What's the second line of Oh Little Town of Bethlehem? Where did Christmas trees originate? In which country did the tradition of hanging stockings originate? What was the name of the angel that visited Mary and Joseph? What lucky item is traditionally found in a Christmas pudding?

Her fingers flew over the keys. When she accidentally mistyped a reindeer's name, the screen beeped and the question stayed on screen until she'd amended her answer. The quiz obviously didn't let a contestant continue if they'd answered wrong. Her heart skipped along and she realized she was actually enjoying this. She just wished she hadn't lost those few seconds when she'd panicked at the beginning. Her eyes couldn't help but keep glance at the timer as she tried to answer more and more questions.

Finally it counted down the last few seconds.

Three…

Two…

One…

When the buzzer sounded, she sat back and glanced at her final score. Most of the questions had been straightforward. There were only a few that might have proved tricky to the average person. But not to Lara Cottridge.

She bit her lip. Three days. The radio station would announce the ten finalists in three days. After which, there would be a live on air quiz. That was bound to be a bit more challenging. She grinned and headed over to her bookshelves, pulling out some of the more obscure Christmas books she owned.

It was time to start studying.

Lara had ten thousand dollars to win.

BEN BLINKED. WHAT? He yanked his feet down from the coffee table, and leaned over the laptop. Since when had this been a timed quiz? He'd missed the first ten seconds by the time he finally started typing.

None of the questions were hard, but his fingers sometimes slipped on the keypad. He smiled at the questions. Any average Joe could answer these. There was the odd, slightly more unknown Christmas fact, but his confidence rose with each second that passed. Ben had always had a competitive edge, and this was a reminder about how much he liked to win. How many people would actually enter the contest? The radio station was statewide. More than six hundred thousand people lived in Vermont, and KNWZ was easily one of the more popular radio stations. Competition could be stiff.

His fingers kept going. The good thing about a timed contest was it made things more honest. No time for people to look things up on the Internet. No time for cheaters. But there could easily be people who typed much quicker than he did. He frowned, paying close attention to the screen and concentrating hard.

A few seconds later, the screen blanked out and his score was displayed. Ben sat back and nodded. Maybe he could have done a little better. He toyed with the idea of using another email address to try again, but shook his head. That wasn't his style. Three days—that was how long he'd have to wait to find out if he qualified or not. He'd keep things quiet until then. No point in giving the kids something more to tease him about until he knew for sure.

He pushed the laptop from his knees and stood up. He'd just had an order come in for a rocking chair. It might be late, but he was itching to get started.

There was no time like the present.

❦

"MR. WINTERS! THEY'RE announcing the Christmas quiz winners at five PM. Did you enter?"

Ben had half a mind not to tell the truth, but what would that teach the kids? "Yeah, I entered."

"What was your score?"

He tapped the side of his nose. "That's my secret. But why don't you bring the radio out to the main gym hall and we'll listen to the announcement together?"

His stomach gave a little squirm and he almost laughed out loud. He was *nervous*. Ridiculous!

Sure enough, a few moments later, the smooth voice of the announcer sounded.

The Christmas Quiz has been our most popular contest ever. Twenty thousand—yes, twenty thousand of you registered to try our online quiz. The questions were randomly generated, so, for those of you who tried to play with multiple email addresses, it wouldn't have helped much. But never mind that! We had a whole range of scores. Who knew how many—or how little— answers a person could squeeze into two minutes? Our scores ranged from zero to…well, you all are about to find out. We'll announce our top ten winners—without giving their scores away. After that, we'll call them all to get them live on air, letting them answer questions live until we're down to two winners. And watch out, folks… If you don't answer your phone, we'll just take the next contestant in line. Our top ten will only have five seconds to answer each question. If they take longer then…eh-oh! The announcer made some weird noise. *Yep, they'll be eliminated. So, here we go, folks—our top ten high scorers are…*

The kids crowded around the radio, all leaning in as if it could make them hear more clearly.

The announcer started running down the list of names. *Jill Smith from Burlington; Ira Banner from Randolph; Mary McLean from Island Pond; Ben Winter from Briarhill Falls…*

The voice faded away as the cheers erupted in the gymnasium.

"You did it! You did it, sir!"

Four of the kids jumped on him at once, sending him tumbling to the floor. Doubled over in laughter, he missed everything else the announcer said.

Part of him couldn't believe it. He'd made it through.

It seemed like the celebration was turning into a pile-on—of which he was currently at the bottom of a very large pile of kids. Struggling to breathe, he choked out, "Okay, guys… Get off me. Let me find out who the other contestants are."

They were still laughing as they slowly moved off him. There was a noise in the distance. One of the girls screamed, "Your phone… Your phone… You've got to answer it!" She ran toward the office before Ben even had a chance to pick himself off the floor.

His brain was scrambled. She was right. There *had* been something about answering his phone in a certain period of time. Last thing he wanted was to be eliminated through dumb bad luck.

Alisha ran back, his phone in her hand and she shoved it at him. His finger swept the screen while he prayed he wasn't too late. "Ben Winters," he said, trying not to sound breathless.

❧

LARA COULD HAVE heard a pin drop in the office. At ten to five, all computers had been switched off and everyone had downed tools. Even the laughter had stopped.

Every co-worker had asked time and time again what her score was, but Lara had kept tight-lipped. A few had admitted to trying themselves, but only scoring ten or twelve. Those scores were making her nervous. She'd tried to work out how quickly answers could have been typed, but the random stuff had confused her. What if someone else hadn't needed to type the names of all the reindeers? It didn't seem entirely fair.

She swallowed the lump that had appeared in her throat. "Why aren't they telling us what everyone scored?"

Abby tossed her hair over her shoulder. "Because they

don't want the rest of the finalists to be intimidated. Imagine that one guy who might have scored ten more than the rest of you. You might all just give up."

"Makes it more interesting," Rae agreed.

"Listen up," said Barb said as she plunked herself down in the seat next to Lara. "Here it comes."

Lara twisted her hands in her lap. Part of her wished she were listening at home, but the girls hadn't taken no for an answer, and said that they all had to listen together.

They'd already insisted there would be drinks afterward – either conciliatory or celebratory.

The announcer started listing the names. "Wait!" Rae shouted. "That was someone from Briarhill Falls! Can you believe it?"

Lara blinked. She hadn't really been paying attention to where people were from. As soon as she'd heard the start of each name—and knew it wasn't hers—she'd began waiting for the next one.

She paid more attention.

Lance Evers from St. Johnsbury; Heather Goodwin from Plymouth; John Brown from Glover; Jennifer Johnson from Montgomery; Ira Westfield from Fair Haven...

How many was that now? She hadn't made it. Her gut was twisting. She had to keep a neutral face. She couldn't let them see how disappointed she really was.

And finally, our last contestant is...Lara Cottridge from Briarhill Falls. Did you hear that, folks? The whole state of Vermont and we've got two contestants from Briarhill Falls.

Amazing. They must like Christmas in those parts.

Cupcakes and cookies were tossed into the air around her. Screams cut through her thoughts, but her brain was still too focused on what the announcer said. She was having a tiny bit of trouble breathing in.

"Lara!" Arms went around her, enveloping her in a variety of bear hugs.

"You did it, girl!"

"We knew you could do it!"

Her office chair spun around as everyone grabbed for her. She was still catching her breath as her phone started to ring.

It was muffled, trapped somewhere at the bottom of her bag.

Rae's voice cut through the merriment. "Quiet!"

Everyone froze.

"Phone, Lara, where's your phone? You need to answer that."

Still disorientated from the spinning of her chair, she floundered. There were too many bodies around her. She couldn't even *see* her red barrel bag.

"It was there," she said, pointing to an empty gap in the floor space. "I was sure I'd left it there."

Five people scrambled around the floor on their hands and knees to check under chairs and desks, as the phone still distantly rang in the background.

"Got it," Abby screamed, thudding it onto the desk next

to Lara's.

For the first time in her life, Lara was cursing the use of her favorite Christmas bag. It was a unique brand some people called them picture bags, a Christmas scene was stitched on the front of the leather bag. This one showed a snow-covered street with shop fronts, decorated Christmas trees, and people walking past in winter clothes. It really was her favorite, but as her hand dug around the bottom of the bag, frantically trying to find her phone, it started to slide off her favorite list. Why had she used this one today? It was huge. Small animals could get lost in it.

"Come on," her colleagues shouted, making the panic in Lara's chest press even deeper.

Finally she felt the little shudder of the phone reverberating next to her fingers. She grabbed wildly and yanked it out, sliding her finger across the screen, and pressing it to her ear in one movement. "Hello?"

There was an achingly long silence. She'd taken too long. They'd cut her. Then finally, she heard a voice "Lara Cottridge?"

"Yes…" Her reply came out in kind of a squeak—in a voice she didn't recognize at all.

There was a strange, high-pitched noise in the office.

"Oh, you'll need to turn your radio off. It can cause negative feedback."

She signaled frantically to the girls. "Turn it off."

Rae ran over and flicked the switch on the radio. The

faces around her fell. Now they couldn't hear what was happening on air. Lara put her finger to her lips and switched her phone on speaker. "Not a sound," she mouthed silently.

"Hi," came the cheery voice. "Congrats on being one of our Christmas Quiz finalists. In a few minutes, you'll be live on air. All you need to do is answer the questions they ask you. No bad language now! And you only have five seconds to answer—any longer and you'll be disqualified. Do you understand?"

Lara nodded before realizing the person at the end of the phone couldn't see her. "Yes, of course."

"The questions are random. If anyone gets a question wrong, they don't get through to the next round. We'll keep going until we only have two of you left."

Abby bounced on her toes. Her mouth was moving, but Lara had no idea what she was trying to say. A few seconds later, Abby grabbed a piece of paper and pen, she scribbled. *I'm taking the radio to the other room. I'll tell you when people drop out.*

A few girls put their thumbs-up. Before Lara had a chance to think about anything, Abby disappeared with the radio and Rae stood in the doorway between the rooms.

Lara crossed her legs. She hadn't needed the bathroom all day, but, of course, had an overwhelming urge that it was time to pay a visit right now. She pressed her lips together, and told her brain to concentrate on one thing only. Now was not the time for distractions.

She had a quiz to win.

THE GYMNASIUM WAS bedlam. The kids wouldn't stop whooping, no matter how much he kept trying to tell them to calm down. The woman from the radio station at the other end of the phone kept laughing, telling him to get somewhere quiet so he could hear the questions. He flicked off the radio as instructed, then backed into his office and closed the door. The window still looked out over the gymnasium, showing the twenty faces pressed up against it. One of the kids waved their phone at the glass, signaling they were streaming the radio station. Phones were normally barred in the gymnasium, but Ben could hardly enforce that right now. And it was good they were excited. Truth was, he was a little excited now, too. He ignored the butterflies, reminding him that the last thing he wanted to do was the let the kids down.

One of his most important roles as a coach was to always encourage the kids to try. Even if they didn't win.

He kept repeating this mantra in his head. His competitive streak was edging out already. Ben Winters didn't like to fail—no matter how valuable the lesson.

He sat down on the chair, shaking his head at the faces pressed in front of him. It would take more than a little elbow polish to clean that glass.

Rory —one of the kids—started jumping up and down again, pointing toward Ben just as a voice came over the speaker. "Okay, Ben Winters, are you ready for your first question?"

He sat a little straighter. "I am."

The host paused for the briefest of seconds before asking, "In which city do thousands of people make their way to Christmas mass on roller skates?"

He answered without even thinking. "Caracas, Venezuela."

"Well done," the host said. "I'll come back to you in few minutes."

He heard the line click. The kids were jumping up and down again. Okay, these questions were a little tougher than the ones online, but still seemed fine. Rory shook his head a few seconds later and made a signal holding up one finger, then drew it across his neck.

Ben laughed. He had to assume that someone had just got a question wrong, and not that his student was about to murder someone.

Nine. Nine people left. He could do this. This might actually be okay.

LARA DIDN'T WANT to lean forward. She was pretty sure her

shirt was sticking to her back. She hated feeling uncomfortable, but nerves were definitely getting the better of her. Her bladder felt like a swimming pool, and whatever it was she'd had for lunch that day was making its presence known.

"Now, Lara," the radio announcer said, making her jump.

"Yes," she said quickly.

"Your question. Which country has a festive legend about a giant cat roaming the snowy countryside?"

"Iceland," she said quickly, breathing a sigh of relief.

"Correct," the host enthusiastically said. "I'll get back to you soon."

Lara took another few breaths. This might be okay. All she had to do was keep her cool.

Rae gave a thumbs-down from the doorway. Someone must have gotten their question wrong. Lara couldn't pretend she wasn't a little glad. At least she wasn't going to be first to drop out.

It seemed like no time at all before the host was back. "Now, Lara, next question—in which country is it considered lucky to find a spider's web on your Christmas tree?"

"Ukraine." She didn't hesitate for a second, and Rae silently clapped her hands in applause.

"Well done, Lara, back soon."

She was starting to get excited now. Two questions down. This might even be fun.

It seemed to take longer to get back to her this time. Rae

ran forward with a sticky note in her hand. *Commercial break.*

Lara winced. Didn't they realize just how nervous their contestants might be? A few minutes later, the host was back. "Lara, next question, can you name the recognized symbol of Christmas in New Zealand?"

For the briefest of seconds, Lara had a complete mind blank, almost as though she hadn't really understood the question. Then, pictures flashed into her mind—of trees with gnarled roots and bright crimson flowers. "The pohu-tukawa tree," she shouted.

There seemed to be a pause. Maybe she'd taken longer than five seconds? She held her breath until she finally heard the voice. "Correct!"

Lara sagged back into her chair, her stomach growling loudly. Rae started to wave one arm, still keeping entirely quiet. She slowly held up one finger, then another, then another. Oh my. Another three contestants gone? The questions must be getting *way* tougher.

Six left. She just had to hold her nerve.

She couldn't help but start drumming her fingers on the desk. Rae signaled another person out, right around the time Lara's mouth became inexplicably dry.

"Next question, Lara!"

"Okay," she answered without thinking.

"What's Santa's zip code?"

Lara frowned, wrinkling her nose. "HOH HOH?"

It was the first time she'd actually wavered. This one might actually be an old wives' tale.

"Correct!"

The next question seemed to come around much quicker. Rae held up her hand and mouthed, "Only three left."

Three. Lara had almost done it. She'd almost made it to the final. The last thing she wanted to do was fail at the final hurdle. Not when she was this close.

"Lara, who was the first president to put up a Christmas tree in the White House?"

"Franklin Pierce," she said, the words shooting out of her mouth in pure relief. She absolutely knew this one.

"Well done," came the reply.

A few seconds later Rae started bouncing on her toes.

The host came back on. "Well, that's it, folks—we have our two finalists!"

❦

BEN HAD DONE his best to pretend his hands weren't clenching into fists the whole time as he tried his best to focus on the quiz. The kids he coached watched him through the glass panel in his office. From questions about Krampus, Befana, the Italian witch, and Dutch children leaving their shoes out, it seemed that plenty of his Christmas muscles had been stretched.

Rudy, one of his school kids, had got more teasing as

time had gone on. He'd started moving off to the side of the glass panel, grabbing himself around the neck when another competitor got eliminated. He'd made a couple of plays of pretend heart attacks and other similar acts as the contestant numbers went down and down.

Finally, he ran clean across the gymnasium floor and did a forward flip, causing Ben to stand so quickly his chair had toppled over. "No mat, no flip," he yelled automatically, hand slamming against the glass.

But Rudy landed perfectly, with both thumbs up, just as the host came back on the line.

"Congratulations, Ben Winters. Folks, you're not going to believe this, but out of twenty thousand competitors across the whole state of Vermont, it turns out our two finalists both come from the same mountain town of Briarhill Falls. Can you believe it, folks?"

Ben couldn't believe it. He took a few steps back while the kids larked about outside in celebration. To be honest, he wanted to join them. He'd never seen their grins quite so wide. It was nice to have something to celebrate together.

The host kept talking. "So, go on, you two. Tell me, are you secretly holed up together, planning how to win every Christmas quiz in the universe?"

Ben wasn't quite sure how to answer that one. He had no idea who the other competitor was.

Then he heard a nervous laugh. "Of course not," a distinctly female voice said. And even though he should never assume, she sounded young.

"Let's find out a little more about our finalists. Lara, you first."

He could sense the nervous pause before the other person finally spoke. "Well, I'm Lara Cottridge. I'm twenty-six, and I work in the hospital admin department."

There was a loud array of whooping and cheers in the background. It was clear her colleagues had supported her the same way his kids had been supporting him. Twenty-six. He frowned. The name wasn't familiar.

"How long have you lived in Briarhill Falls, Lara?" the announcer asked.

"I moved here a few years ago," she said, her voice a little high. "To be close to my grandma. I used to spend the holidays with her every year when I was a kid—so I'm very familiar with Briarhill Falls. She lives in a local retirement home here now. I'm hoping to win the money to help give the gardens a makeover."

Ben inwardly groaned. Of course he'd known any other competitor would have a cause that was equally as worthy as his own.

"What about you, Ben? Tell us a little bit about yourself."

He tried not to heave in a huge breath. He wasn't particularly keen on telling the world about himself. The last thing he wanted was pity. But as he turned to the gymnasium, he could see twenty expectant and enthusiastic faces on him. He also couldn't tell any lies.

"I'm Ben Winters. I'm thirty, and I've lived in Briarhill Falls most of my life."

"What do you do?"

"Hold on a sec," he said as he opened the door. "I have a few friends who want to say hello."

As soon as he opened the office door, the kids let out a roar, much louder than the one Lara's colleagues had managed.

"Oh my goodness," the host exclaimed. "Who on earth do you have there?"

Ben laughed. "I coach at the high school, and that's where I am this afternoon."

"You work at the high school?"

"Oh no, just volunteer here as a coach."

One of the kids leaned over and shouted, "He used to be a pro baseball player!"

Ben cringed as the radio host jumped all over that statement. "You're a professional baseball player?"

"No, no," he said quickly. "Well, I was, for about five minutes. But I got injured." He hated sounded like he was making excuses. "I had a change in profession. I'm a carpenter now and own a woodshop in Briarhill Falls."

"Oh…" He could almost hear the deflation of interest in that single word. But the host did her job. "So, yes, well, so how does an ex pro-baseball player, a current kids' coach, and a carpenter end up as the king of Christmas trivia?"

He wasn't quite sure how to answer that one—at least not in the punchy way a radio host would want. "Who doesn't love Christmas?" seemed the easiest way out.

The host let out a sharp, false laugh.

"So, if you are lucky enough to win the money, where will it go?"

That question was much simpler. "That's easy. It would go to the school. The gymnasium could use a new floor."

The kids cheered all around him, making him feel a little less self-conscious.

"I'm curious," the host said. "Lara, Ben, do you know each other? Just how big is Briarhill Falls?"

"No." They seemed to speak in unison. Though Ben *was* already curious about his competitor. He had half a mind to walk past the hospital admin block to see if anyone was celebrating.

Lara spoke, her voice still had that nervous edge to it. "Briarhill Falls isn't that big. Around thirty thousand people. But it's a popular ski resort, and the population always swells during ski season."

"Well, folks, it looks like you two will be meeting sometime soon. KNWZ will be heading up to Briarhill Falls! We'll set up the next tasks in your quest to win ten thousand dollars." She gave a long pause, obviously trying to build some tension. "Are you ready?"

The kids around Ben erupted, drowning out whatever Lara's reply might be. He couldn't stop smiling. He wasn't

overly fond of being the center of attention, but if it motivated the kids and kept them excited, then he was glad he'd
taken part.

He gave a half-sigh, "I guess so," he said resignedly as he
picked up the nearest ball, bounced it a few times, and
scored the perfect basket.

Chapter Three

"DOUBLE SHOT VANILLA latte?"

Lara never even got to say her order out loud. She'd been coming to this coffee shop for the last few years, and they knew her order by heart.

The barista folded her arms, then nudged her colleague. "What does she look like today?"

The guy glanced over his shoulder as he filled the coffee group head and pressed the buttons to start the machine. "It's a blueberry muffin kind of day."

The barista shook her head, "I was thinking a blueberry scone."

Lara smiled as she pulled her wallet from her purse. They teased her like this every single day. "One of these days, I'll order a completely different drink, and I'll pick something random from behind the counter." She pointed to the glass counter, which held a whole host of bakery beauties. She tipped her head to the side and said, "But today, I'll have a blueberry scone."

"I win!" The barista smiled as she lifted a set of tongs and put the scone in a paper bag. The door chimed, behind Lara and she turned as a tall guy walked in dressed in sawdust-covered jeans and a thin cotton long-sleeved shirt. The snow was lying thick outside. The guy must be freezing.

"Here he is. Mr. Double espresso and bagel with cream cheese and bacon."

Lara gave the guy a smile. "Glad they're treating you the same. I don't feel so picked on now."

The guy looked over and gave her a polite but casual smile as he walked past—coming close enough that she caught a glimpse of green eyes and the muscles defined beneath that thin shirt.

"Best coffee in town," he said as he pulled some money from the back pocket of his jeans. "Almost makes the bad jokes worth it."

Robbie turned around, from the coffee machine setting two drinks down together. "Hey, weren't you two on the radio yesterday?"

Lara's hand froze as she reached to pick up her cup.

She turned to face the guy next to her, noting he'd mimicked her actions.

"You're Ben?"

"You're Lara?"

They stared at each other for a moment, both wide-eyed. Her brain went into overdrive. Why couldn't her competitor look like a wretched, spotty, short-ass kind of guy? That way he'd be much easier to hate. Instead, she had the guy who looked like he'd just walked off the pages of a catalogue. Tall, with dark rumpled hair and broad shoulders. She was pretty sure he'd fill out those jeans well.

She tugged at the collar of her wool coat self-consciously. There hadn't been time to think about her appearance this morning. She had too much else on her mind. She'd just picked up the first winter coat in her closet. This red one was fine, but the random pink and pale blue scarf she'd paired with it didn't exactly match, nor did her purple leather gloves.

He moved before she did, holding his hand out toward her. "Well, Ms. Cottridge, I guess it's a pleasure to meet you."

She hesitated for a second before pulling her hand from her glove and accepting his grasp. Calluses. She could feel them straight away with his strong grip. Of course. He was a carpenter. He worked with his hands every day. His hand swamped hers, sending interesting little tingles shooting up to her shoulder.

"Ben Winters," she said, grinning broadly, she tried to temper it down. She was acting like some kind of fan girl. "It's nice to meet the competition."

There was an instant gleam in his eye. He obviously liked this kind of talk.

He kept shaking her hand, not loosening his grip at all. "Yeah, the competitor, that's me. A fount of complete and utter useless Christmas trivia—at least, that's what the kids tell me."

"Yeah, I heard them yelling in the background. You've got quite your own little cheer squad there, haven't you?"

His fingers started to release her hand. "I guess I do." He smiled then, as if he'd just been lost in a memory.

"So what happens next then?" Ken, the barista, leaned across the counter toward them. He glanced from one to the other. "I can't believe you two don't know each other. You're both in here every day."

"We are?" Lara was surprised. She'd gotten to know a lot of the regulars in the coffee shop with her frequent stops.

Ken folded his arms, looking pleased with himself. "Regular as clockwork."

He gestured to one of the tables. "Hey, why don't you sit down and swap strategies? This quiz thing is going to be fun."

Fun? Her stomach gave a disloyal twist. It wasn't supposed to be fun. It was supposed to be a means to an end. A way to give a little back to her grandmother's care home. Now, she was up against an ex-pro-baseball player with looks like a model, and a charity heart that he practically wore on his sleeve now he'd told the radio station listeners he volunteered as a coach at the high school. She just prayed this didn't come down to public votes. How on earth could she hope to have any kind of chance against a guy who could clearly win every popularity contest? She might even be tempted to vote for him herself.

"Sure," he said, it came out in a lazy, sexy kind of drawl.

"I have five minutes."

Those words prickled at her—as if that were all the time he could spare. And he still had that amused kind of look in his eye. Was he planning on making fun of her?

She glanced pointedly at her watch. "Okay, five minutes. I have to get to work soon."

He wrinkled his nose and said, "It's Saturday."

She raised her eyebrow. "Oh, that's right. Hospitals close on the weekends."

He gave the slightest nod of his head. "Of course, sorry." The easy shrug of his shoulders. She wasn't quite sure if he'd meant to cause offense but it was clear he expected to be forgiven.

He pulled out a chair, gesturing with his hand for her to sit. She had half a mind to pull out her own chair, but that would just be petty, so she sat at the small round table, setting down her coffee, but keeping her blueberry scone firmly in her lap. Last thing she was going to do was eat her one luxury of the day in front of her competitor. Some things were private and for her enjoyment entirely alone.

Ben obviously didn't feel the same way about his bagel. He took a large bite, chewing and swallowing quickly.

"So..." he said with a smile. "Tell me about your grandma."

It was just as well she was already seated because the question threw her. "W-what?"

"Your grandma? Which care home is she in? You said on

35

the radio, you were doing the contest for her."

"Oh, I am. It's not a care home exactly. It's residential—assisted living. She has her own small apartment, with assistance if she requires it. It's safe. It means there's always someone there."

Lara gulped, realizing how much those words meant to her. She licked her lips, willing her eyes not to fill up. "She didn't want me to have to stay with her. She had a few falls and…." Her voice trailed off for a second as she couldn't quite finish it. "Anyway," she said, far too brightly. "She opted to move into the residential home. She thought it was more practical. There's shared communal space too where she can socialize if she wants, and the place has beautiful gardens – or at least it did."

She was talking too much, and she knew that. Ben watched her carefully with those oh-so-green eyes. "What happened?"

She pulled a sad face. "The contractor disappeared—along with all the funds. We think he might be in Hawaii, or even as far away as New Zealand. But it's all just rumors. No one actually knows. The home can't afford to lay out that money again this year. They're all budgeted out. They have to keep funds for adaptions or repairs if they're needed."

Ben's forehead creased. "Gardens in Briarhill Falls? It snows around five months out of the year here. How much can they do in the gardens?"

Lara felt herself bristle. It was almost like he was saying it was a worthless cause. "Christmas is a special time in the residential home. They always have a giant fir tree. The whole complex is built around a large, open hexagonal courtyard that's surrounded on all sides by glass. It's full of winter boxes, heathers, evergreens, with some benches and alcoves. Even if someone isn't well enough to go outside, they can still enjoy the outdoors."

"And they can't have the fir this year?"

So, he *was* listening. She shook her head. "No, it's one of the biggest expenses. And the tree decorating ceremony is one of the nicest events because everyone gets to take part. The residents pick their color theme every year." Leaning forward conspiratorially, she lowered her voice. "You have no idea how bad the fights over the color can get. It always ends up like the War of the Roses."

She blinked. She'd leaned too much. And he didn't move. Now, she could see the tiny lines around his eyes and a few freckles over his nose. Trust a guy to have that gorgeous, tanned skin she'd always wanted. Without thinking, she breathed in. There it was, that earthy, sawdusty smell, mixed with a little cologne. He smelled exactly the way she thought he might.

His lips turned up in a broad smile—almost like he could currently read her thoughts. She jerked back, fumbling with her hands in her lap and knocking her bagged scone to the floor.

They both bent down at once to grab it, heads clashing.

"Ow," she cried out.

"Ouch!" he said, rubbing his head as he straightened, her paper bag in his hand.

※

THE HEAD IMPACT wasn't the only thing Ben Winters felt.

He was kind of wondering where she'd spent the last few years hiding, because if he'd come across her before—he would have remembered.

But no matter how much he scoured his brain, he just couldn't place Lara Cottridge at all. She was cute. Nope. She was very cute.

Her cheeks were flushed so pink they almost matched her coat, and her dark brown eyes matched her hair. There was a definite aroma of peaches in the air. Normally, he could assume it came from the coffee shop bake counter, but after that clash, he had direct evidence it was coming from that glossy hair.

She seemed a little nervous. And he wasn't quite sure whether it was from being around him, the contest, or whether this was just her.

Lara had the kind of face that could make hearts bleed the world over. Thank goodness this was a radio contest and not a television one—he wouldn't stand a chance. He was curious about her job at the hospital, and even though she seemed nervous now, at first meet, he'd seen a real spark of fire in those eyes. Competing against Lara Cottridge could be interesting.

"Are you okay?" he asked.

She nodded quickly. "It's fine."

He leaned his elbows on the table, getting a little closer. "So, you want to win for your grandmother and her friends. Just how big of a Christmas fanatic are you?"

She gave him a careful glance—almost as if she were weighing him up in her head—wondering if he would be a worthy opponent.

She gave him a one-word answer. "Plenty." It was like she'd just drawn a line in the sand—or the snow.

Her eyes narrowed just a fraction. "So, what's your story? How did you end up coaching at the high school?"

He shifted a little. He'd preferred it when the focus had been on her. "I came back here. Did some training, then took over the woodshop from Mr. Elderbank. One day, a kid came in, wanting a present for his mom." He took a breath, he didn't really like telling this story. "Anyhow, he recognized me and said that their regular coach had just had a heart attack, then asked if I could help out. They had a game coming up, and they needed some coaching."

"And you agreed just like that?"

He shook his head. "Oh no. Coaching wasn't even something that had ever entered my brain. But this kid was persistent. He came back every day." Ben smiled. "I thought he liked the woodshop—or he just wanted to supervise me making his gift." He shook his head and the smile vanished, "But I found out things were tough at home, and since his coach was gone, he didn't have practice as an excuse anymore."

Lara's eyes widened. She looked shocked. "What was wrong?"

Ben pressed his lips together. It didn't matter it had been a few years ago—he wasn't going to betray a confidence. News traveled in small towns, and sometimes people could be identified from just a few words. "Things were just hard. He'd signed up for every team, so he would have practice every night after school. He just needed a little time out, a little space—like a lot of teenagers. When I realized that…" He let his voice tail off.

"You agreed to coach?"

He nodded. "The irony? I might have rocked at baseball, but I'd never been great at basketball or football, but I learned to love them."

"What about your injury?" He could see a hint of curiosity on her face.

His hand went automatically to his shoulder. "Oh, I had surgery years ago." He winked at her. "Not every part of me is genuine now." He couldn't help but smile as her cheeks tinged pink. "As long as I don't overdo things, I'm generally fine."

She leaned her head on her hand as she sipped her coffee. "But how on earth do you do all that? Run your own business but still coach every night?"

He shrugged. "I keep my own hours. I stop work in the late afternoon, spend a few hours at the school, then head back to the shop and work into the evening."

"What does your family say about that?"

Now it was his turn to be surprised. Was this her way of asking if he were married or in a relationship? His brain silently cursed himself for not asking her that question first. His eyes went automatically to her hand. No visible ring. But that didn't mean anything.

He gave a casual shake of his head. "No family in town anymore. My parents moved to Florida a few years ago." He gave a laugh. "Turns out that after more than sixty years in Vermont, they decided their bones needed a little sun."

"Oh." He sensed she wanted to ask something else. A bit like he did. But it seemed neither was going to ask the partner question.

She straightened a little. "So, what does the school need money for again?"

He leaned back in his chair. "Nothing smart, nothing sexy. Just something completely essential. A new floor."

Her brow creased. "There's something wrong with the floor?"

He held up one hand. "It's okay, but it's pretty worn in some places. It doesn't have much life left in it. It's time for a refresh."

He saw a glint in her eyes and wondered if she was about

to say something cheeky.

"Do it," he said without thinking.

Her eyes did a quick scan around them before her lips edged upward "I was just wondering how many parts of you might need refreshing?"

"Ouch!" He punched his fist to his chest. He laughed. "If I'd said that to you, I would be wearing your coffee."

She nodded in agreement. "Probably."

She licked her lips and took a deep breath. "Ben, just so you know, I'm serious about this. I really want to win."

He was a little surprised by her change of tone. "You think I'm not?" He felt automatically defensive.

She shook her head. "No, no, of course not. Why put yourself through the stress of the live quiz if you weren't? I just mean even though I understand you wanting to do something for the kids, I'm not just about to roll over." Her cheeks flushed again as she realized what she'd said. She held up a hand. "No, what I mean is, I guess I want this just as much as you do."

He blinked. She was looking straight at him with those toffee-colored eyes. He wasn't quite sure what to think about Lara Cottridge. He was willing his body to ignore the little pulses currently going haywire.

Was Lara used to getting what she wanted?

Something prickled. Was he getting played?

That thought chilled him, more than the temperature outside. Ben had experience at being played. He'd almost been played right out of his bank account and last property when he'd signed his first big contract. All by an incredible actor with a pretty face. He'd vowed never to let it happen again. Every part of him was instantly on edge.

He looked straight at her. "You know, the kids have a whole host of reasons for coming to practice. Sometimes, it's company, sometimes it camaraderie, sometimes it's just taking part, sometimes it's a safe place." He tapped his fingers on the table. "And only sometimes, it purely because of the love of the sport. So, I won't walk away and just hand you this prize, Lara. My kids need it just as much as your grandmother—maybe more."

He could see the tiny flash of annoyance sweep over her face immediately and she took a sharp breath. He tried not to focus on the fact her chest had just puffed up beneath her fitted coat. She stood, grabbing at the scone to stop it from falling again. "I can assure you that my cause is every bit as worthy as yours."

He leaned back, his initial feeling of being played not quite so fierce anymore. Instead, he let his amusement sweep over him. He folded his arms across his chest. "I'm sure it is."

She was still clearly annoyed. "And I'll do all that I can to make sure I win for the retirement home. They deserve it. After working hard all their lives, they deserve a nice garden and a cute courtyard. It's not too much to ask, it is?"

Her voice had got a little louder and several heads in the

coffee shop turned to look at them both. Ben shifted uncomfortably under the stares. He had no reason to be here anymore. His coffee was done, his bagel was finished, and he'd met the competition. He just wasn't entirely sure what to make of her.

The sense of being played dangled in front of him once again. He just couldn't quite shift it. Particularly when there were numerous sets of eyes of him.

He stood, pasting on his best smile. "Neither is a gymnasium floor for the local kids who want to keep healthy and learn to be team players, is it?"

She blinked, glancing around and realizing they had an audience.

She tilted her chin upwards to him, her tongue was firmly in her cheek as she held her hand out to him. "What was it they said—may the best Christmas nut win?"

For the second time that day he took her hand in his and shook firmly, while nodding his head. "May the best Christmas nut win."

Chapter Four

T HE CONTEST WAS all anyone in the office had talked
about for the last three days. Doctors, nurses, and
patients regularly stopped her in the corridors to wish her
well or give her their latest bit of Christmas trivia in case it
would help her out at the next stage.

Trouble was that the radio station hadn't exactly been
specific about *what* the next stage would be.

All she knew was she was to turn up at the mayor's office
in the town center tonight. She tugged at her navy-blue shirt
decorated with a few sequins. She'd bought it years ago
because she thought the pattern looked like Christmas
baubles and she loved wearing it. The radio host had told her
to wear something festive—if she had it. Lara had almost
laughed out loud. No one could do festive clothes like she
could.

Or at least she'd thought. Until she stepped into the office and saw Ben standing smiling, with a Christmas sweater
complete with crackling fire on the front.

She couldn't help herself and walked straight over. How
on earth could it do that? Her finger automatically poked at

his chest, hitting something hard. "Your phone?"

He nodded and pulled it out from a hidden pocket in the sweater. "Isn't it cool?"

"Hmmm," was all she could bring herself to reply.

Marty, the radio host, was standing with a microphone. He gave a wave of his hands. "Equipment is all ready, so we'll start broadcasting live in a few minutes. Don't be nervous," he said with the ease of a guy who'd spent years talking on air. He pointed to the corner. "And we'll do a bit of live streaming, too, for the people who might be watching online."

"What?" Lara gulped. Now she understood why they'd told her to wear something festive. She should have thought of this. She looked sideways at Ben. He still had that big grin on his face, confidence seemed to abound from him. He wasn't the slightest bit unnerved by the thought of being streamed online.

She did a silent count in her head while she rubbed her damp palms on her jeans.

Marty gave her a nod. In a way only an older man could without causing offense. "Love your shirt. You look cute."

"Too bad I didn't bring my own flaming fire, though." She sighed. Ben's sweater was much more festive than her sparkly t-shirt. His would look great for the online viewers. She really, really wanted to win this, but her head told her that if she was online, already she'd want to vote for the cute guy.

Marty pulled a face and waved his hand. "Don't you bother about that. You're beautiful just as you are."

She pressed her lips together as she prayed nerves wouldn't get the better of her. Already she felt a little swamped. After her parents had died a few years ago, she knew she was the only person left to look after her grandma. She already felt guilty for not looking after Grandma herself. She'd put her career plans on hold and took the first job that she could find in Briarhill Falls so she could be close at hand. It was a lucky break that the job at the hospital was so great. Lara's supervisor had already suggested putting her in the management trainee program. But Lara still felt as if she wasn't doing enough for her grandma. Hours at the hospital were long, and she couldn't always visit every evening. Maybe winning this money could lessen the guilt she felt a little.

Marty paused for a second and glanced between her and Ben. "You know what? You two would make a nice couple." He nudged her. "Just think, maybe KNWZ will get their own matchmaking wedding!"

She took a step back and shook her head straight away. "A wedding? Are you crazy? I barely know him." She stared at where Ben was talking to one of the other crew members, she rolled her eyes. "And I don't even like him." It was her attempt at a joke. Who wouldn't like the gorgeous, charming guy? She often spoke quickly when she was nervous, and Marty immediately jumped on the statement.

"What?" Marty's eyes widened. She could practically see the excitement on his face. "Well, if you don't want to give me a wedding, maybe you could give me a war?" He gave a thoughtful nod of his head, "That might make even bigger headlines."

Panic flooded through her. How had she managed to get herself in the middle of this crazy conversation?

"What? No. Scratch that."

But the expression on Marty's face told her everything she needed to know. She could almost see the plans formulating in his brain. She looked frantically to Ben, who had no idea what had just happened. She kind of wished she were wearing his shoes—he seemed so cool, calm, and composed—even though he must feel the same pressure she did. She'd have to warn him that Marty had some crazy ideas—without, of course, letting him know they'd inadvertently come from her.

Marty gave a wave of his hands. "Get ready, folks. We're good to go in, five, four, three, two, one..."

It was like someone flicked a switch somewhere and Marty moved into professional mode. The words just seemed to flow easily from him. And this wasn't a scripted radio or TV show. There wasn't a teleprompter with words on a screen that he could just read. No, this guy did everything from scratch.

He was actually really gifted. He seemed to understand that most listeners would be on the radio, so he described both Ben and Lara and what they were wearing. He also described their surroundings and gave a little bit of background about Briarhill Falls. Lara couldn't help but smile when she saw the mayor in the corner rubbing his hands, thinking about additional tourist opportunities.

But Marty also had a great twinkle in his eye as he joked with the staff member live streaming what was going on. He introduced a few people around the room before he finally settled on Ben and Lara.

And that was when it all started to go embarrassingly wrong.

"Well, folks, we have our two finalists here, and take it from me, we couldn't have dreamed up a more handsome couple. Do we think there could be a hint of romance in the air?" Marty's voice dripped with innuendo while Lara—thankful to have a tiny bit of warning as to where his thought processes were going—managed to keep her face as neutral as possible. Ben, on the other hand, looked as if someone had just hit him over the head with one of his tools. This was totally unexpected for him.

She saw him swallow and paste a smile on his face, trying to recover from the initial side wind. But it was too late. Her gut gave a little twist. A romance with Lara had obviously never crossed his mind—not even as a wide possibility. That much was clear. And she couldn't help but feel a little stung.

It didn't help that she knew how completely and utterly ridiculous that was. Trouble was, even though she was now trying to deny it, a few errant thoughts about Ben *had* flitted through her brain. Now that just felt immensely embarrassing. It wasn't like anyone could see into her brain, but it didn't matter. *She* knew, and that was enough.

Marty shoved his microphone into Ben's face. "So, what do you say, Ben?"

Ben paused, obviously trying to find suitable words. "Well..." he said slowly. "I think Lara..." His gaze met hers "is a very beautiful young lady." he finally answered.

The fact he'd taken so long to find them made those nice words sound like an insult.

Marty snaked across the room to Lara, putting the microphone opposite her lips. "And you, Lara? What do you think about this great guy?"

Lara kept her face perfectly blank "I hear he makes nice furniture." she said in her best non-committal manner.

A crease appeared in Ben's forehead. Then, he raised his eyebrows. It wasn't in surprise. It seemed more like a challenge.

For the first time, Marty seemed a little thrown. "Well, there we go, folks, Ben makes nice furniture. For those of you who need to know." He gave Lara a look that made her cringe. It was clear he'd wanted her to play along...and she'd just ruined his game.

But Marty was too experienced to be put off for long. "So, maybe there won't be romance, folks. Maybe Briarhill Falls is a lot more serious than that. Maybe this challenge will bring out our finalists' competitive streaks. Wouldn't that be interesting? I mean, what would *you* do to win?"

The live stream camera was facing her, so Lara tried not to pull a face. Marty made it sound like they might commit a crime. She might think about it, but she wouldn't actually do it.

Marty positioned himself between her and Ben. "So guys, you must want to know what the challenges will be? We want you to know that the producers at KNWZ contemplated *lots* of things for these challenges." There he went again, emphasizing words and implicating things that made her wonder what on earth she'd done.

Please don't let it be rappelling down a cliff or doing a black diamond ski run, she thought. Up until this point, she honestly hadn't been too worried about the next challenges. Yes, she'd been curious, but she hadn't really expected anything too difficult.

Marty clapped his hands together. "So, each challenge is very different. There will be five challenges over the next ten days. They will test different skills and talents—maybe some our finalists didn't even know they had. And the most important part, people—the KNWZ audience will get to vote for the winner."

Oh no. A popularity vote. If viewers went online and got even a glimpse of Ben, he would definitely get the lady vote—both young and old. He had that good-guy-but-sexy look about him, the working man with a glint in his eye that women of any age seemed to adore.

Plus, he worked with kids. She might as well give up now.

But something still burned deep inside. That fly away comment. As if her cause—her grandmother and her colleagues—weren't quite as worthy as his high school kids. That still rankled. And she hadn't forgotten it. He obviously hadn't met someone like her. A guy who looked like Ben— particularly one who'd been a pro-baseball star—was probably used to women swooning at his feet and doing whatever he pleased.

Well, Lara Cottridge wasn't that girl.

She gave Marty her best smile. "Well, I'm ready for the challenges. I think they'll be my favorite part."

Marty smile widened. "Well that sounds like fighting talk to me."

She kept her smile as she nodded, determined not to look over at Ben. "They just might be."

Marty whipped around to Ben so fast Lara had to stop herself from bursting out laughing. "So, Ben," he pressed his microphone back up to Ben's mouth, "Do you think you have a skillset that will match Lara's?"

She could almost see Ben cringe. Why did everything that came out of Marty's mouth seem like some kind of double entendre?

Ben gave her a calculated glance. He had his arms folded across his chest, emphasizing the defined muscles under that crazy sweater. She sent up a silent prayer that most of the people of Vermont were listening right now, instead of watching. When he spoke, his voice seemed a little lower than before. Sexier. "I think..." he glanced at her and licked his lips. "I think each of us will have our own special skillsets. I guess it'll be up to the listeners to decide who does what things best."

Darn him. She hated the way he was looking at her right now. As if he actually meant to tease and torment her. A guy should be locked up for looking at a girl like that.

Marty looked delighted "You're absolutely right about that Ben." He pulled a red envelope from his back pocket. "And here we have it, folks. The first challenge. It will be announced..." He paused for a second. "Right after this song and these advertisements."

There was a signal from one of the other team members, and Lara could only imagine someone had flicked the switch to start the tune.

"We need to wait?" she asked.

Marty shrugged. "It's radio. We have to play songs, you know, and keep the advertisers happy. Where do you think the prize money is coming from?"

Of course. She knew that. But patience wasn't exactly her biggest virtue.

Ben seemed entirely too laid back for his own good. He chatted to everyone around him while she paced, waiting for the song to finish and the task inside the envelope to finally be revealed.

She'd thought she was fine about all this. Happy, relaxed, and definitely not nervous. But all of a sudden, she felt the urge to be sick on her shoes.

Before she had time to find the nearest bathroom, Marty was talking again.

"So, if you're listening, you'll hear me tear open the envelope. If you're watching the live stream, you can watch it now." He made a big show of waving the envelope around. Like on every show in the world there was the longest drumroll. It seemed to last forever. Lara resisted the temptation to snatch the envelope from his hands and open it herself.

Finally, with a rip, he tore the edge of the envelope off, then pulled out a gold card. "Here we have it, folks. Oh, interesting." He looked at Ben, and then at Lara, nodding slowly.

"Anytime this year," she heard Ben say under his breath. Thank goodness he was obviously a bit nervous, too, and just as anxious as she was to find out what the challenge might be.

"So folks, the first challenge takes place right here in Briarhill Falls at this time tomorrow night. The first thing we'll ask our contestants to do is...decorate a Christmas cake!"

Just at that one of the staff wheeled out a trolley and whipped off the large cloth that was resting over the top of it, revealing two round plain white iced cakes.

"We have here two identical Christmas cakes, and nothing else. Our challenge for our competitors is to find the appropriate accessories and accouterments to decorate their cake live on air tomorrow night. They'll do it right here, for thirty minutes with no assistance from anyone else. They can bring in whatever they like, but they have to do it all alone. When they're finished, we'll put pictures on our website, and you'll all have twenty-four hours to vote for your favorite."

Lara didn't know whether to laugh or cry. She could bake fabulous cookies, loafs, and traybakes. But cakes weren't really her specialty. She wasn't the most artistic person in the world, but she had seen some spectacular Christmas cakes. Ideas already buzzed through her head. Anyone could buy cake toppers like tiny Christmas trees or sleighs, but it was the people who thought outside the box that decorated the kind of cakes that made people suck in a breath when they saw them.

She looked over at Ben. He seemed kind of stunned and looked down at his hands. His giant hands. She grinned. This task might be too delicate for him. Even though she'd never done it before, her smaller hands might give her the edge.

She beamed and clapped her hands together. "Sounds fantastic. Can't wait."

BEN GROANED WHEN he woke up. His dream had consisted of ten thousand individual one dollar bills flapping like butterfly wings as they floated out the window.

He'd spent most of the wee hours of the morning online. Then he'd watched some cable show where a professional cake maker generally put the rest of the world to shame with his spectacular creations.

Lara's enthusiasm had been hard to ignore. She might even have looked a tiny bit smug. She expected him to do poorly at this challenge. *He* was expecting him to do poorly at this challenge.

He glanced out at the white world outside. He had to pick up supplies. But the thing was, he wasn't entirely sure what he *needed* to pick up. He still hadn't decided on a design, and although there were shops in Briarhill Falls, it wasn't like living in a city where you could more or less find anything that you wanted. Online shopping wasn't any use either. Nothing had same day delivery, which was what he needed right now.

He rolled out of bed and started the coffee. He couldn't spend all day on this. He had work to do. Those chairs wouldn't put themselves together. He washed and dressed and flicked on his computer. Pouring himself some coffee and sitting down at his own table with a pad and pen in front of him.

His hand automatically ran over the grain of the wood on the table. It had been one of the first pieces he'd made, and yes, there were imperfections. But that was the joy of working with wood. Maple, walnut, cherry, and oak, all grown in Vermont. He was big on sustainability, always convinced customers that home grown was best. He glanced up at the computer and blinked at the number of emails in the woodshop inbox. Sixty-six? Normal was around twenty a day. He started to scroll through them, wondering if he needed to change his junk mail filters.

But no. Or maybe...yes.

Some of these were genuine requests about furniture or other hand-carved items. Some were... He squinted at the screen. What exactly did you call these? Fan mail? They were mainly from women. Chatty, but quite personal emails. One in particular made his cheeks flush as he read it. Others were random, a little kid who'd sent him a photo of something he'd carved in school, saying he wanted to work with wood, too. Ben flagged it—he'd answer it later. Another was from a guy he'd played baseball with on the pro circuit. They'd lost touch a few years ago and Lucas had heard Ben on the radio and wanted to know how he was doing.

That was nice. Things might not have worked out for him in the major league, but he had good memories. He leaned back in his chair, trying to ignore just how tired he actually was. There were a couple of stores he needed to visit. He'd looked up cake decorating equipment on the Internet, and naturally didn't have a single thing he might need. He'd also need to buy a huge amount of powdered sugar and food coloring so he could practice mixing and piping. It might be best if he tried not to look like a complete fool tonight.

He'd printed some pictures he'd found online last night and he spread them out across the table. He still hadn't really decided what his design would be. Part of it might depend on what was in the stores in town. The videos he'd watched last night had slightly terrified him. It was people with art in their blood and skilled hands. They'd made it all look so easy.

Ben sighed and stood up. Cake decorating was never going to be his thing. But maybe some of the other challenges would be. He didn't want to give up without a fight.

Ben grabbed his jacket and boots. No time like the present.

⁓❧⁓

LARA HADN'T BEEN able to concentrate at all at work today. All anyone could talk about was what she planned to create tonight. It seemed that every single individual she met in the hospital all had a whole stream of ideas, and all were apparently experts. That tiny bit of confidence she'd had last night was slowly but surely ebbing away.

She'd cheated a bit by buying three plain cakes so she could practice decorating before she had to attend the main event. As she pushed open the door to Mrs. Oakens' store, the heat hit Lara square in the face. The place was stifling.

Mrs. Oakens sat happily behind the counter, wearing two winter cardigans. Lara unbuttoned her wool coat and slid it off, depositing it in the corner of the store. She only had forty minutes for lunch, so she needed to move quickly. She grabbed a basket and waved to Mrs. Oakens. "Hi, just grabbing some things."

She glanced at the thick blue parka already on the chair, wondering who it belonged to. It was an odd little store—part groceries, part craft supplies, part haberdashery. She wandered down the first of the cramped aisles just as – in slow motion – a head rose up from the aisle behind.

"Well," came a deep voice. "What a surprise to see you here."

Lara started. Darn it. She tried not to seem surprised as she kept her eyes firmly on the items on the shelves. "I could say the same to you." She lifted her head. "I don't believe I've ever seen you in here before."

Ben did his best to look indignant. "I'm in here all the time."

Lara smiled, as she looked at Mrs. Oakens. Everyone knew that the old woman was partially deaf and wouldn't be able to hear a single part of this conversation. "So, I take it you two are on first-name terms?" she asked teasingly.

He gave her an aghast look. "Of course not. My mom would be horrified if I called Mrs. Oakens by her first name. It's hardly polite." He leaned forward, and whispered with one eyebrow cocked, "And in case you were wondering, it's

Ellis."

She couldn't believe he actually knew it; she tried to hide her surprise. She, too, had always called her Mrs. Oakens. Lara bit the inside of her cheek as she realized there wasn't a single thing on this aisle she could use. She walked around to the next one but almost stumbled when she saw how full Ben's basket was.

"What are you doing?" she pointed and shook her head. "It looks like you just emptied the entire shelf in there." The basket was crammed with powdered sugar, food coloring, piping bags, nozzles, and a whole host of different tiny ornaments, along with some random Christmas decorations. The more she looked, the more envious she became.

"Maybe I did." he smiled. "But I figured I would just buy everything and decide what I need later." He moved swiftly down toward the cash register, almost as if he didn't want her to study his basket any further. Lara glanced at her watch and started to panic, mimicking what she'd just accused Ben of doing by throwing things randomly into her basket.

Like Ben, she still hadn't decided on her theme. For some crazy reason, she hadn't expected him to practice as much as she did. So finding him in here had unnerved her. She gave a nervous glance. He was standing talking easily with at the counter to Mrs. Oakens while he packed his bags. Mrs. Oakens was looking at him with adoring eyes, clearly flattered by whatever he was currently saying.

Lara grabbed a few more things and headed to the counter where Ben tucked the last items into his bags. He tucked the brown bags against his chest before giving Mrs. Oakens a nod. "Thanks for all your help. See you later."

He inclined his head just the slightest before heading out the door. Mrs. Oakens gave Lara a broad smile as she started to ring through the items. "Such a nice young man, isn't he?"

"I don't really know him," Lara answered. "We never really crossed paths before."

"Really? What a surprise." Mrs. Oakens patted the high-backed chair she sat on. "He custom built my chair, you know. Designed it at just the right height so I could sit comfortably behind the counter and keep my eye on all the customers." She tapped the edge of her nose, and Lara glanced behind her at the now-empty store.

"That's great," she conceded as she packed up her items.

But Mrs. Oakens was still talking, "And his Christmas cake sounds like such a dream, doesn't it? Everyone loves a ski slope in Vermont."

Lara froze. Not quite sure what to say. She was almost certain that Ben wouldn't want to her to know this information. But it was too late now.

She gave a broad smile as she handed over her money. "Thanks so much, Mrs. Oakens. Have a nice day." She waved as she hurried out the door.

A ski slope? Lara could beat that.

Chapter Five

H E'D FINALLY MASTERED it.

No. Not entirely true. He'd finally managed to construct a ski slope above the white cake *and* decorate it without the results looking like a complete disaster. It was rolling the darn icing to cover the slope that was the tricky part. But lumps and bumps were a natural part of a ski slope? Hopefully, he could get away with it.

As he walked into the mayor's office tonight, he could feel the tension in the air. He'd been told he could invite a few people to cheer him on—so long as they knew they couldn't participate. Three of the kids were standing nervously near the entrance-way and rushed over to meet him. "Are you ready, Mr. Winters?"

He nodded. "As I can be."

Rudy pointed to the other side of the room. "That woman has been there for ages. Look at her table."

Ben turned and looked. It was like something from a cake show. Mixing bowls, spatulas, food coloring bottles all neatly lined up, and even a strange-looking kind of spray can. What on earth was she creating?

"Never mind, guys," he said as casually as he could, pretending not to notice as Lara turned around, catching her hair and tied it back from her face with a red ribbon.

The ribbon matched her dress—bright red and covered in Santas. He'd forgotten. He'd forgotten the instruction about festive clothes.

He shrugged off his jacket and wrapped a spare piece of tinsel from his bag around his neck. It would have to do.

Marty hurried over. "Good, you're here. You can set out your accessories, but not prepare anything beforehand. Everything must be done in front of the studio audience."

"Audience?"

Ben looked to his right. It seemed like Lara had brought along some of her work colleagues. A few of them still had their hospital IDs around their neck. There were also some other people—a few from Briarhill Falls, but some others that he didn't recognize.

For the first time, Ben had a twinge of nerves. It had been a long time since he'd felt anything like that, and the realization made him smile.

All he had to do was not make a fool of himself.

"It'll be great," Christy said, tugging at his sleeve. She looked so hopeful. Rudy and Rory had similar expressions on their faces. The kids had actually pulled tickets to see who got to come with him tonight. This meant a lot to them. Ben had to do his absolute best, even though he wasn't entirely sure how this would go.

Marty was still talking, "I'll introduce you both, recap the challenge, and then you can begin." Marty beamed, obviously quite excited by this. Ben thought back to the emails he'd gotten today. Even though he'd only been on the show for a few minutes, he'd already reaped the benefits. What kind of impact could this be having on the radio station?

Ben moved into position and stared down at his items on the table. They weren't quite as neatly arranged as Lara's. She was right next to him. He could see her concentrating fiercely on her items, her fingers on one hand tugging at the side of her dress. She was nervous. She might have initially seemed calm, but she was just as nervous as he was.

That made him feel slightly better.

Marty gave a thumbs-up and started talking into the microphone. "Good evening, folks, and welcome to KNWZ's Christmas contest!"

LARA TRIED SO hard to concentrate, but her brain whirred. Standing next to Ben Winters wasn't helping. She hadn't realized that their tables would be quite this close.

He just seemed to have some kind of 'presence'. She could smell his aftershave drifting towards her, along with some kind of soapy scent – probably his laundry detergent. Either way, the fresh scents seemed to be mixing with the other Christmas aromas in the room. Her whole body had a nervous buzz around it. Two out of three cakes she'd decorated earlier had been a complete disaster.

That couldn't happen tonight. It just couldn't.

The microphone appeared under her nose. "So, how are you feeling about the challenge tonight, Lara?" Marty asked.

She moved into professional mode. "I'm really excited. Looking forward to it," was her automatic response. At the last minute, she remembered to look up and smile at the person filming, too, giving a quick wave of her hand.

Marty moved over to Ben. "How about you, Ben? How do you feel about cake decorating?"

Ben didn't smile quite so widely as before. He gave a casual shrug of his shoulders. "What can I say? My hands aren't quite as delicate as Lara's, so she might have an advantage, but I'll try my best."

He looked over at her, his green eyes connected with hers. There it was again. That weird little buzz. For a moment, she couldn't break the connection—she didn't *want* to break the connection. He gave her the tiniest smile, and she blinked.

Maybe he was trying to distract her.

That thought made her pull her shoulders back and straighten her spine. Cake decorating. For thirty minutes, all she had to think about was cake decorating. How hard could it be?

Marty waved his hands. "Let's count down, folks. Three,

two, one, and *go*!"

Lara focused. Immediately grabbing her paper template and food coloring. She'd spent most of the afternoon trying again and again to cut a template that would allow her to wrap around the cake, then brushed over with food coloring, then pulled back, transforming the sides of a cake into a brick wall—or, more importantly, something that resembled a chimney.

Ben had pulled out a plastic-wrapped piece of cake—was that a shop-bought madeira cake? He started to carve parts of it off with a knife. What on earth was he doing? After less than a minute, he dumped it onto the top of the round cake. Her brain sparked. A ski slope. This must be his mountain.

She felt a small wave of panic. She needed to concentrate on her own cake. She pulled out the ready-made fondant icing and started modeling, shaping parts that would be the top of the chimney and Santa's upside-down legs.

She'd found the design online yesterday. It had looked fantastic, and had lulled her into a false sense of security that it would be easy to make. But this afternoon had taught her a valuable lesson—things were frequently much harder than they looked.

She couldn't help but glance in Ben's direction once again. He, too, had pulled out a readymade fondant sheet, which he laid over the cake.

Darn it. His idea looked much easier to construct than hers.

She concentrated again on the colors. Red for Santa's legs with a white trim at the bottom, then the thick black boots. The square chimney was finished. All she had to do was stick the upside-down Santa in there. A quick glance at her watch told her she had five minutes to spare. She grabbed some random colors of leftover fondant, she started shaping some square parcels.

There was a flash next to her. Tinsel. Ben was wrapping tinsel around the edge of his cake. Why hadn't she thought of that?

His ski slope was lumpy and bumpy because he hadn't managed to smooth it properly, but it actually looked good—just like an actual mountain. He had a few small ski figures that he positioned randomly on the slope, with an upside-down sled at the bottom. He reached for some other spare parts of icing, obviously intending to do something else, but his hand brushed against the bottles of food coloring and sent them all flying.

Ben jumped back as the colors pooled on the table. It was like slow motion. One of the bottles—of dark blue—catapulted into the air and flew directly at Lara.

She didn't have time to move, even though her brain screamed at her to. She watched, mouth open, as the liquid stream from the bottle and landed all over her red dress. The dark blue stain blotched outward, spreading like some kind of giant virus.

"Oh no, I'm so sorry. I'm such a klutz." She hadn't even

had time to move before Ben was right in front of her, kneeling down on the floor and dabbing a cloth to her dress. His face was directly opposite her abdomen.

For the briefest of seconds, she couldn't actually move. It felt like being stuck in some kind of time warp. But the incessant dabbing of his hand against her now-damp dress quickly brought her to her senses.

"Eeeewwww." She pulled the dress from her body, sure the dark blue food coloring would likely already have stained her skin. That would make for a fun shower tonight.

Ben lifted his head, and looked right at her. His pupils widened—in horror at realizing his actions might be a tiny bit inappropriate?

He jumped and stepped back, inadvertently backing into her table. She watched in shock as – the slow motion feed seemed to appear from nowhere again – as one of Santa's legs fell sideways from the chimney.

"Darn it," he hissed under his breath.

"And we have less than a minute left." Marty's voice broke into her thoughts. "Oh dear, what's happened here?"

He swept over next to them and glanced at both tables, eyes fixating first on the pool of food coloring swimming on Ben's table, then on the dark spreading stain on Lara's dress.

She opened her mouth to say something, but Marty kept talking, and she realized the question hadn't really been for her.

"Oh dear. There's been a *calamity* over at the cake decorating tables."

Even though she was still in shock herself, she couldn't help but smile at the way he emphasized the word for the listeners at home. "It seems that Ben has had a bit of spillage, which managed to impart some damage to Lara's fantastic Christmas dress." He glanced at his watch. "But oh, salvage what you can, people. We're on a ten-second countdown. Come on, folks, count with me. Ten, nine…"

Lara jumped forward. Grabbing a piping bag, she squirted a large bit of icing on the bottom of Santa's leg before pushing it back into place. She held her hand as steady as she could. The icing had gotten a little stiffer, and she prayed it would be enough to hold the leg in place when the countdown finished.

True to form, a few seconds later Marty finished the countdown. "Three, two, *one*. Hands off, folks. Let's see what we've got!"

Lara's hand shook as she ever so gently released it from the leg. It stayed in place. She wasn't entirely sure how long it would stay there, but even a few minutes would be long enough.

The people in the room cheered and crowded around the two tables. Ben's ski slope actually looked okay. The cake board might be surrounded by food coloring, but the actual slope was still white and adorned with the upside-down ornaments. It was simple but effective.

Marty spent a few minutes describing Ben's cake in detail

to the listeners at home, then asked a few of the people in the room what they thought of it. The whole time, Lara stood holding her dress away from her skin. Ben's eyes kept flitting toward her.

Lara wouldn't look at him. She wouldn't. Not only had he ruined one of her favorite dresses, but he'd also nearly sabotaged her cake. Anyone would think this was entirely planned.

A horrible sensation crept over her skin. But she didn't have time to dwell on it before Marty was at her table and began describing her cake. "This one is a real beauty, folks. Lara has managed to capture Santa stuck up the chimney, or, in this case, when Santa got stuck *down* the chimney. His legs are sticking out of the chimney with presents scattered all around. She's even managed to decorate the base of the cake to look as if it's made entirely of bricks." He gave her a beaming smile, "What does everyone think?"

Lara stepped backward to let other people get a closer look. Everyone was enthusiastic and she felt a little swell of pride. Practicing *had* paid off.

Marty kept chatting, explaining that photos of both cakes would be up on the radio station's website and votes would be open for twenty-four hours. At the end of that time, the votes would be counted and the winner of the challenge announced, along with the next task.

Lara lifted her hand and leaned against the wall. She was exhausted. What on earth had she signed up for? Another, what, eight days of this?

A few minutes later, Marty signed off the air and the room seemed to settle down. Ben was instantly surrounded by the kids who had come along with him. Lara's workmates started chattering loudly, trying to decide what bar they should all go celebrate in. Rae moved over to Ben and shot him one of her winning smiles. "Hey, rival, want to come and have a drink with the competition?"

The words were laden with innuendo, and Lara cringed. Ben's eyes shot to the three teenagers around him. "That's nice, but no thanks. I'm just going to see these guys home, then come back to tidy up."

"Your loss." Rae waved her hand and came back over. "Right, who's ready to hit Skier's Woes?" Lara shook her head. The bar was popular around here with both the locals and the tourists, but she was just too tired to face it.

"Not for me, thanks. I was up late last night, and I need to catch up on my sleep."

Rae leaned forward. "You were up late?" Her wicked gaze glanced in Ben's direction. "Mixing with the enemy, perhaps?"

Rae's voice was louder than Lara liked "Of course not," she quickly said. "I was searching for a design idea. And we've got work in the morning." She took a deep breath and sighed, touching her dress. "Let's face it, I'm not really dressed to go anywhere. I'll need to go home and soak this to see if I can get the stain out."

Rae tutted and looked at the stain. "Honey, that's never gonna come out."

Lara gave a reluctant sigh. "Probably. But I need to try. I love this dress."

Rae waved her hand. "Well, if you change your mind, you know where we are."

It was surprising how quickly the room emptied now that the show had finished.

Before she knew it, Ben appeared back at the main door after seeing off the high school kids. Only the two of them were left now.

The empty hall seemed to echo around her. It wasn't warm in here, but all of a sudden she felt hotter than before.

Ben made an exasperated noise as he looked at the remaining mess on his table. before shooting her half a glance. He tried for a few seconds to mop up some of the spilled food coloring before dumping the cloths and walking over to her. "You know, your Santa cake is really good." He tipped his head to one side. "Clever."

She was surprised at his admission. "Thank you," she said, the words coming out a bit reluctantly. She looked over at his ski slope. "Your ski slope was...surprising."

There was a hint of a smile on his surprised face. "Why?"

She paused for a second, wondering whether to be honest or not. "Because it was simple but effective. It does pretty much look like a ski slope."

He laughed out loud. "You didn't think I could do it,

did you?"

Lara bit her lip and nodded her head slowly, admitting it to them both. "Let's just say you've…" She struggled to find the right word. "Surprised me," she decided.

"Oh, I've surprised you?"

"Yeah," she admitted before she turning to face him. "You might have a chance of winning the public vote."

"You think?" Now it was him that looked surprised. He shook his head. "Mine is a lumpy downhill ski slope. Yours is…" He gestured with his hand. "Much more skillful."

Lara folded her arms as she looked between both cakes, her skin prickling. She wasn't sure what it was about being in an enclosed space with this man that just seemed to put all her senses on red alert.

His cake wasn't half bad at all. She was going to have to admit it. But what about those who'd watched online—those who'd seen the full Ben Winters experience? The guy was hunky. He was handsome. He was rugged. It was like a triple threat. And now he'd just tried his very big hands at cake decorating to win something for kids in a high school. He was like the regular TV movie hero. Hell, she might even vote for him herself.

She gave him a half-smile. "Sometimes, people don't want skillful. Sometimes people like simple." She touched the edge of his cake. "You have the disaster ski slope with everyone tumbling down it. People might like that. It'll appeal to their sense of humor."

"And Santa stuck upside down in the chimney won't?"

She turned back to her own and her spirits lifted a little. It *was* funny. It was also quite cool. But it was also clear to see the work that had gone into to it. "You should have seen versions one and two. They didn't look nearly so good," she admitted.

"What, did you practice all afternoon?"

"You didn't?"

He pulled a rueful face. "I still had some coaching to do this afternoon, so I couldn't practice as much as I wanted."

Part of her was glad he was taking this seriously. And part of her wasn't.

Her competitive edge was sneaking further and further out. She really did want to win. It would be so much easier if this were all just a big joke to him.

He pointed to her dress. "And I'm sorry about the dress. If you tell me where you got it, I'll replace it. I'll get you another."

She shook her head. "I got it last year. The store won't have anymore." Something struck her just as she said the words out loud. "You know, if I didn't know any better, I'd think you were trying to ambush me."

The thought had appeared out of nowhere, but even in a few brief seconds it started to grow wings in her head.

"Over a cake decorating contest?" he asked, his tone was indignant.

"Maybe you thought a clumsy stumble would send my cake splatting to the ground?"

Even as she said it, she knew it wasn't a nice allegation. She tried to keep her tone part joking, but that little spark in her head wondered if there could be some truth to it. Would Ben really do something like that?

"Or maybe I just wanted to make Santa navy blue?" Ben said, a hard edge to his words.

The atmosphere between them had changed in an instant. And it was all her fault. Or was it?

"Maybe you did. Maybe you want to win at any cost?"

"That's ridiculous."

"Is it?"

"I don't need to play dirty to win. I can beat you in this contest fair and square."

"You think?"

He folded his arms across his chest. "I know."

Lara picked up the rest of her supplies, then dumped them into her bag. "Well, in that case, Mr. Winters, show me your best hand. I can beat it anytime."

He shook his head. "Don't count on it."

She grabbed her jacket, not even waiting to put it on. "Good luck with the vote. I'll see you tomorrow night. Good night." She flounced out, but she just couldn't help it. Ben Winters seemed to know just how to push her buttons.

"Good night," he said smartly behind her as she walked out and slammed the door.

She stopped for a second, and leaned against the door and closed her eyes for a second. "Baseball," she whispered. "*Anything but* baseball."

Chapter Six

H IS FINGERS WERE sore from voting on his phone. He'd also made up a few emails addresses so he could vote online. It was pathetic, really, but Lara Cottridge had annoyed him when she'd accused him of cheating.

He wrinkled his nose for a second uncomfortably. So what exactly was this then? He'd even emailed a few friends from out of state to persuade them to vote for him, and he'd put the voting link on his Facebook page.

He groaned and leaned his head on the table. "What have I done?" he muttered. "She's turning me into the kind of guy that I hate."

He'd drawn the line at asking the kids to vote for him— even though most of them had already told him that they had.

He glanced at the clock, and grabbed his jacket, his heart kind of sinking as he shrugged it on.

After last night, his enthusiasm had waned a little. He didn't like that things had gotten a little ugly between him and Lara last night. Ben wasn't that guy. He had never been that guy.

He hadn't liked what she'd accused him of, but it wasn't an excuse to all out challenge her.

He trudged down the street toward the mayor's office, which was beginning to feel like a makeshift radio station. All day today, the station had been publicizing the contest telling everyone to listen in tonight to find who had won the first challenge and what came next.

Marty practically jumped on him as soon as he walked through the door. "Good, you're here. Why did you leave it so late?" He glanced over his shoulder. "Makeup!"

Ben stepped back. "What? This is radio, Marty. What are you talking about?"

Then he noticed the sheen on Marty's face as the host shot him a perfect-toothed smile. "But it's also live streaming. Apparently, you both looked a bit pasty last night, so we're going to do something about that."

A girl rushed over, a big brush in her hand, and grabbed Ben by the sleeve. "Quick, over here."

Ben let himself be led over to a chair. It took him a few moments to realize that Lara sat in the other chair. She was wearing a bright green dress with a red scarf around her neck. Festive colors. It suited her. Her face was also an unusual shade of pale orange.

"Ben." She gave him a brief curt nod.

"Lara." He grimaced as the girl came at him with a sponge. "Am I going to be the same shade of orange?" he whispered.

The girl smiled. "Honestly, you'll look normal on camera. And we can take it off right after."

"Is that a yes, then?" She gave the briefest of nods then started smearing something onto his skin with a sponge.

❧

LARA TRIED TO pretend her stomach wasn't flip-flopping everywhere. She hadn't slept last night. Her conscious had been pricking away at her over the unfair accusation.

She never should have accused Ben of trying to sabotage her. It had been a cheap shot, showing her own insecurities.

She just really, *really* wanted to win. And for one mad, crazy second, she'd thought his stumble might have been deliberate.

But Ben Winters didn't strike her as that kind of guy. And she was pretty sure she must have plummeted in his estimations.

She stood up from the make up chair and caught her orange glow in the mirror. *Ugh.* Hardly attractive, but what did she know about TV makeup?

She moved into position behind last night's cake as instructed and pasted on a smile. Ben had managed to clean up well. His table was spotless with only the cake left with a few miniscule splatters of food coloring that were hardly noticeable.

Marty moved into position, wearing a red velvet jacket

tonight. "Welcome, folks, to KNWZ. We've had lots of votes for our Christmas cake decorating contest. Just over twenty thousand so far. It's been our most successful competition ever, and we want you all to stay with us. So, if you haven't already voted, you have five minutes left. Boys against girls. Head on over to our webpage and decide which cake you like best, then press the button. Yes—it's as easy as that, folks. Then hang on and listen to some music. We'll be back with you soon."

Lara blinked as a large light flickered on next to her. When Ben moved into place behind his cake, her stomach started to somersault. Two of her workmates had come along tonight. The office had spent most of their lunch hour all voting for her, and it had become a little embarrassing.

Ben waved to three students who'd arrived. Different ones from last night. They were practically bouncing on their toes.

Marty's voice broke into her thoughts moments later.

"Well, folks, that's it." He moved between the two tables. "We want you to know that only a few hundred votes separated our entries." He gestured one way, pointing to Lara's cake. "So did you vote for Santa," he turned to Ben. "Or did you vote for our ski slope?"

One of the production assistants walked over with an envelope, then placed it in Marty's hands. "Here we are."

Lara blinked. The envelope was gold, actually gold. And then she noticed Ben's face. It looked pale beneath the orange glow. He gripped the edge of the table. He was nervous. Mr. Cool, Rugged, and Handsome was actually nervous? Parts of her insides turned to mush before Marty's voice jolted her back to attention.

"I have the envelope, and I'm pulling out the results. Drum roll, please."

Someone pressed a button, and a drumroll filled the air. Marty dramatically pulled the card out and Lara resisted the temptation to lean sideways and peek at the result.

Her heart hammered in her chest. All the tiny hairs on her body stood on end. There was an invisible pet in her stomach doing gymnastic routines. *Hurry up. Hurry up.*

It was like watching one of the many TV shows where the host gives a dramatic pause before announcing the winner. Marty had learned his trade well.

For a few moments, there was strange expression on his face. What was wrong with the card? It was like he was struggling with something, but then his face lit up and he beamed again. "Well, folks, I want you to know this has been a close race. There were only," he paused again, "five hundred and thirty-two votes, between our two competitors."

Lara swallowed. He'd originally said there was over twenty thousand votes. That meant that across Vermont—winner or loser—around ten thousand people had voted for *her*.

She was stunned. She was nobody. She was a small-town girl—a hospital secretary—and yet, ten thousand people had either picked up their phone or logged onto their computer to vote for her cake.

She gripped the edge of the table to stop herself from swaying.

"And the winner is…"

She blinked, expecting the pause this time. But she couldn't help it, her eyes connected with Ben's. He looked every bit as nervous as she did, but that didn't stop his lips from edging upward as he gave her a half smile.

"Lara Cottridge!" Marty appeared in front of her, all shiny teeth and big microphone, which he shoved towards her. Her friends started yelling and cheering. Across the room, she could see the disappointment on the high school kids' faces as they reluctantly gave her a few claps.

"Congratulations, Lara! How do you feel?"

Every single word she'd ever known left her brain. There wasn't a single one left.

Marty's eyes widened slightly, and his face gave a little twitch as he tried to urge her on.

"I'm stunned," she finally said. It seemed the most natural response.

"Well, listeners, she certainly seems that way."

He moved swiftly over to Ben and put the microphone in his face. "Commiserations, Ben, but be happy, because," he looked at the card, "Nine thousand seven hundred and eighty-five people loved the ski slope and voted for your cake."

Lara still hadn't found words, but Ben seemed to have

enough for them both. It was almost like his professional face slid into place as he put his hand to his chest. "And I thank every single one of you. I know it wasn't the best entry, but it was done with heart."

Lara swallowed. Oh boy, he was good.

Marty realized that, and kept going. "So, you're not too disappointed?"

Ben shook his head, smile on his face. Was Lara the only person who noticed it didn't quite reach his eyes?

"Of course I'm disappointed, Marty, but this is just the first challenge. There are four more." He looked over at Lara. "I have plenty of time to play catch up." There was a slight teasing tone in his voice.

One of Lara's workmates made a whooping noise. "Sounds like fighting talk," she shouted good-naturedly.

"Absolutely!" Marty agreed, jumping right on the bandwagon. "So, let's listen to our advertisers and we'll be right back to announce the next challenge. Stay with us on KNWZ."

❧

BEN COULDN'T PRETEND he wasn't disappointed. His heart had lurched when he'd watched both Caleb and Trudi's faces fall as they'd heard the announcement. He'd let them down, and he hated that.

But his short time in baseball had taught him well. Everyone who'd been signed to the team had done their obligatory media training. Keeping a smile in place, staying calm, not showing any negative emotions, and turning any negative into a positive message. These days he hadn't expected his training to serve him so well.

The kids crowded around him, and he put an arm around both of their shoulders. "Sorry, guys. Maybe the next one."

Lara's reaction had surprised him. She'd looked as if she'd had a sudden wave of stage fright. He'd been glad when Marty had swept over to him instead because she'd been painful to watch.

She still looked a bit stunned as her friends enthusiastically crowded around her. The rest of the crew moved into tidy-up mode, clearing the tables, then waving Lara and Ben over to another spot in the room.

They positioned themselves as Marty waited for the countdown to start again. Ben ducked behind him. "You okay?" he whispered to Lara.

She gave a hesitant nod.

"Well done. Your cake was great." He meant it. Her cake had been the best, and he already knew how much time she'd spent on it.

"Thank you," came her whispered reply. "It was close. You gave me a run for my money."

Marty frowned, clearly wanting them to pay attention. "Ready?" he asked pointedly.

They both straightened, fixing their gazes ahead to where the live stream was being prepared.

"And…we're back! So, what comes after cake decorating you might ask? That's a good question. At KNWZ, we want our challenges to take in all aspects of the festive season. Since we're here in snowy Vermont, it would seem foolish not to take advantage of our wonderful weather."

Ben was curious. Surely they weren't going to send them down the ski slopes?

Lara was looking a little pale under that strange makeup, but she plastered a smile on her face.

"So, our next challenge is an outdoor one. What was the one thing we all did as kids as soon as we saw snow outside?"

Marty paused and looked around the room, then threw his hands in the air. "Build a snowman, of course!"

A snowman? Ben smiled. It might have been a few years, but he could do that.

Marty held up one hand. "But, as always, there are rules. Each competitor can select one friend to help them with this task. In two days' time, starting at seven pm, each of you will have one hour to build a snowman in a place of our choosing. The winner will be the contestant who builds the largest snowman in that time. We'll measure them live on air in order to announce the winner straight away."

Ben was grinning now, as Marty turned toward him. Lara might have had an advantage last time, but his size was on his side this time.

"What do you think about this challenge, Ben?"

"Love it," he answered quickly, and honestly, grinning from ear to ear. "I haven't built a snowman in years, but I'm sure one of the kids from the school will be delighted to help me."

He could practically hear the fighting right now about who would get to help. They would all want to do this.

Marty turned to Lara. "And when was the last time you built a snowman?"

Ben watched as she took a deep breath. "Well, it's been a few years for me, too. But when I was a kid, my snowman might not have been the biggest, but it was always decorated the best." Her eyes fixed on Ben's. "I guess we all have to play to our strengths."

It was like another challenge. Another line in the snow.

"And there you have it, folks. Keep listening for our Christmas contest updates. We'll post pictures of both snowmen for you all to comment on—and you can watch the live stream in two nights' time. We might even take a few calls from listeners on how you think they're both doing."

As soon as Marty signed off, one of the assistants rushed over. "Ben, Lara, we're going to need some publicity shots tomorrow, and we might even have a few external interviews."

Ben frowned, thinking about all the work waiting in his woodshop. Last night's emails had been even worse. He didn't even have time to read them all—let alone answer them. He had to prioritize the orders he had rather than take any new ones.

"I'm not sure I'll be available," he said. "I have work to do."

"Me too," Lara said quickly. "The hospital has been great about giving me some flexibility, but I have to keep on top of things."

The assistant's brow furrowed. "These things aren't negotiable," she insisted. "It's all part of being in the contest."

Ben shook his head. He wasn't going to be strong-armed into anything. "Everything is negotiable. Both Lara and I have work—responsibilities. Maybe we could free up some time tomorrow evening. An hour perhaps?"

He looked at Lara and she gave a slow, grateful nod. "That should be okay."

"An hour?" The assistant was clearly far from pleased.

"Sure," Ben insisted. "An hour should be plenty of time to take some pictures and do an interview."

The assistant scowled before, turning and storming off.

"Thanks," Lara said quietly. "She didn't look like she was going to take no for an answer. I can't afford for the radio station to turn up at the hospital. It's just too disruptive."

Ben thought of all the pieces of wood he had positioned around his workshop in a methodical manner that only he would understand. He didn't want strangers in his workplace, either. "I hadn't even thought about that. You think they might just spring up on us?"

Lara looked at the retreating figure of the assistant. She was already on her phone, looking none too happy. "I think she might," Lara said, as she pulled a face. "She doesn't seem to get we might have a life outside of this contest."

SOMETHING STRUCK LARA as she said those words. How much else did she have? Apart from her grandmother and her job, Lara's world had kind of shrunk round about her in the last few months. She'd been so busy trying to keep her grandmother's spirits up that her social life and interests had kind of disappeared. Not that she'd admit it to someone like Ben. The guy probably had the biggest supply of friends on tap at a moment's notice.

"Well, we're not having that," Ben said determinedly. "I'm in the middle of too many projects right now to have photographers moving things around in my workshop. I'm already behind." He ran his fingers through his hair. "Can't get any further behind or I'll end up letting some clients down just before Christmas. There's no way I can let that happen."

He really did look concerned and she had a little flash of what it must be like to be a sole business owner. He didn't have anyone else he could rely on while he took part in the contest. All those customers were solely reliant on him. No wonder he didn't want to get behind.

"How about we meet them on neutral territory?"

Ben looked thoughtfully. "Like where?"

"What about a restaurant? Giuseppe's? Or Pan's Parlour? Or the steakhouse?" she asked, naming the three most popular restaurants in town.

Ben smiled. "Perfect. Which is your favorite?"

She waved both hands. "I don't mind. You pick."

He paused and put his hand on his chin, while he studied her.

After a few moments of silence, she gave a nervous laugh. "What?"

"I'm trying to decide if you're a pork-and-parmesan ravioli, mushroom, bacon, and Monterey jack chicken, or a pepperoni-and-onions pizza kind of girl?"

She was sure her chin just about bounced off the floor. She put her hands on her hips. "How on earth would you know what I like to eat?"

He smiled and shrugged, clearly pleased to have guessed correctly. "So which one do you want tomorrow?"

She thought for a few seconds. "The ravioli. That, and a really good glass of white wine."

"Seven o'clock?"

She nodded as she smiled. "It's a date." Then, she froze. "Oh, no, I didn't mean that, I meant…"

But Ben already had that twinkle in his eye. "A date?" He nodded his head in amusement. "Sure, why not?"

He kept watching her as she babbled. Now that she'd

started, she just couldn't stop. "I just meant—we've agreed on the place and the time—not that it's a date or anything. You know what I mean."

He still had that amused grin on his face. "Oh, I know what you mean. We agreed on a place and a time, so yes, some people might say we agreed to a date."

She stopped talking as heat rushed into her cheeks.

He was enjoying this. He was making fun of her.

"Maybe we shouldn't bother at all?"

"And risk them showing up uninvited?" He let out a laugh. "Lighten up, Lara. Giuseppe's tomorrow night at seven. I'll book it and let the station know where they can find us."

He turned to leave and she couldn't bring herself to find a reply. She was that mixture of embarrassed, tongue-tied, and confused.

She looked over to where she'd already packed up her things. The big box with the cake was sitting at the very top.

"Let's go, Santa," she said as she picked it up. "It's you, me, and a gallon of coffee.

Chapter Seven

I T WAS A strange kind of day. He'd started early, trying to catch up on some of the work he'd missed out on over the last few days. At three, he headed over to the school for some coaching, which mainly ended up being a refereeing match between all the kids who wanted to help with the snowman contest.

It ended up with an agreement to put names in a hat. He didn't want to show any kind of favoritism. He had enough muscles to lift a head onto a snowman by himself, so any kind of help would be a bonus. Ali, a quiet, skinny kid, looked as if he might burst with excitement when his name was pulled from the hat. Ben was kind of glad it was him. Ali frequently stayed in the background, letting the more confident kids lead the way, so it would be nice for him to be the center of attention for once.

By the time Ben finished at the school, it was just after six. He dashed home, jumped in the shower, and grabbed the first clean shirt and jeans he could find, and grabbed a pair of boots.

It had started snowing again. He'd made good time, and

he couldn't help but smile as he strode along the street toward the restaurant. Briarhill Falls was already in darkness, with the glow from the orange streetlights reflecting off the snow on the streets. Some of the shops had Christmas trees in their front windows, lit up by multicolored lights. The whole place looked like something out of a scene from a Christmas card. The streets had definitely been busier these last few days. It seemed like the publicity from the Christmas contest wasn't just helping his business, but those around him, too.

That made him happy. He loved this town. Sometimes in the summer, business slowed down for everyone because the slopes were closed. So it was good to have some extra influx of cash during the winter season.

The yellow lights from Giuseppe's restaurant was warm and welcoming. His heart gave a little stutter in his chest. Dinner with Lara Cottridge. Part of him hoped the photos and interviews would be done in five minutes, leaving the rest of the night for him to get to know his competitor a bit better.

Who knew what tonight would bring?

SHE'D CHANGED THREE times. It was ridiculous. But as she held up yet another dress in front of the mirror, she tried to convince herself this was because pictures would be taken tonight—and not because she would out for dinner with Ben Winters.

She threw the green dress down on her bed next to a black one and a bright blue one. None seemed to be quite right. Too plain, too short, too sexy.

Lara crossed back over to her wardrobe. She needed to hurry. She wanted to have enough time to pop in and see her grandmother before she headed for dinner. She closed her eyes and stuck her hand into the wardrobe, vowing to wear the first thing she pulled out.

Red. A red dress. Last year's Christmas day dress. She'd forgotten about this one. The color was bright and daring, but it reached her knees and covered all the parts it should. There was a v at the front, and a few random sequins on the front, but it wasn't flashy or daring. Would she look like she was trying to impress him?

She hesitated for just a second then glanced at the clock again and pulled the dress over her head, matching it with black leather boots before swiping on some lipstick.

Her red coat seemed like too much, so she grabbed a grey wool coat with a fur collar and some leather gloves. She locked her door before hurrying down the street.

It was more slippery than she'd expected, the fresh snow mixing with some previous ice on the sidewalk.

She could hear laughter as she approached the main sitting area in her grandmother's residential home. "What's going on?" she asked as she went in and sat down next to her grandmother.

"Here she is, our little star!" said one of the other women.

"We're just watching your antics from the other night."

"What antics?"

"Where is he? Did you bring him with you?"

The questions were coming thick and fast, being fired at Lara from all directions.

"Bring who?"

"The hunk, of course!"

Her grandmother was chuckling away. It was the most animated Lara had seen her in a while. She gave a quizzical look at Lara, and then did a gentle tug to the hem of Lara's red dress, which peeked out under her coat.

"All dressed up? Where are you going tonight?"

Lara blushed. "Oh, just doing something for the radio station."

Her grandmother's friend Bess leaned forward. "Something with Mr. Handsome?"

Lara tried to distract them all. Albert, another resident, sat in a chair just to the side, with a few of the others around him. "What are you doing, Albert?"

"Watching you," he answered promptly.

Lara shook her head in confusion. "How can you be watching me?"

Albert's eyes gleamed. "The live stream from the other night. It's on the radio's website." He leaned back in his chair. "We can watch it whenever we like. Steph even put it on the big screen the other night."

Steph was one of the nurses that worked at the home. "You were all watching?"

"Of course we were watching," Jane said, from the other side of her grandmother. "You're doing this for us, aren't you? We want you to win. Have you any idea how many times we all voted?"

Lara's hand flew to her mouth. "You did?" She never would have dreamed of asking, but it hadn't occurred to her they would all vote anyway. But as her eyes scanned the room, she could see many of them holding phones or tablets. She'd bought her grandmother a tablet a few years ago and set it up for her. Lara knew how much the older woman loved it, and it seemed that many of the rest of them did, too.

"Whose helping with the snowman?" Albert asked.

"Probably one of my workmates," Lara said. "I haven't really decided."

Albert gave a little sigh. "Wish it could be me. But my old arms just don't have it in them anymore." He smiled and lifted his arm into a half-hearted bicep curl.

It was like a breeze dancing over her skin. She hadn't really considered needing muscles to for building a snowman. She'd just thought about rolling a big ball and putting another on top. But this contest was all about how *big* the snowman was. She'd need someone strong to help her.

"Can't you get someone strong from the hospital to help you? What about one of the doctors? Or the orderlies?"

She tried to keep her smile in place and not reveal any panic, her brain frantically rattling through all the likely suspects at the hospital. Two of the porters were currently sick, most of the male doctors weren't particularly burly looking, and Ron—the orderly who would probably have fit the bill—had just had a hernia operation.

"I'm sure I'll find someone," she said brightly, making her way back over to her grandmother to pick up her bag. She bent over to kiss her and her grandmother grabbed hold of her hand.

"So, what exactly is going on this evening?"

It had always been the same. It was as if her grandmother could read her mind.

"I told you—some stuff for the radio station, an interview, and some pictures."

But it seemed she couldn't shake her grandmother off.

"And where is this taking place?"

Lara bit the inside of her cheek. "Giuseppe's," she admitted. "Ben and I didn't want the radio station to turn up at our work and disrupt things. It seemed easier to meet them somewhere neutral."

Her grandmother's eyebrows rose with healthy skepticism. "So it's, *you and Ben,* then?"

Lara straightened up quickly. "Of course it isn't. We hardly know each other. I'd never met him before this contest."

Her grandmother was smiling, and Lara knew exactly what she was thinking.

Lara wagged her finger. "And you can stop looking at me like that, right now."

Her grandmother laughed and held up her hands, looking around at her friends in mock surprise. "Looking at you like what, honey?"

They all laughed, and Lara shook her head.

"You're all just as bad as each other." She gave a wave of a hand. "I have to run. See you all tomorrow."

"Lara?" her grandmother shouted as Lara had almost reached the door.

She spun back around. "Yes?"

Her grandmother winked. "You look gorgeous, honey."

A warm feeling spread across Lara's stomach. She blew them all a kiss and hurried out the door. If she'd had any doubts before, she didn't have a single one now. It had been a while since she'd seen all the residents so excited about anything—even if she was the likely object of their teasing.

The clock in the town square started to strike seven, and Lara's heart skipped a beat. She started to half-run, half-walk down the glowing white streets to where the restaurant was.

What if the radio crew had arrived early and Ben had to deal with them on his own? She hated being late. It made her look unreliable.

She was so busy thinking about too many things to concentrate on the slippery mixture of ice and snow beneath her feet. As soon as she came into sight of the restaurant, she took a quick check of the road—no cars—then stepped off the sidewalk and onto the road.

It was like stepping onto an ice rink. Her foot barely made contact with the surface before it shot out from beneath her and straight up into the air. One minute, she was looking down the street—the next, she was staring at the dark sky above and the smattering of silver stars.

❧

HE WAS CUTTING it close. For some crazy reason, he'd started staring in all the shop windows, taking in their Christmas decorations. There hadn't been time for anything like this lately. While it was just him and the quiet street, he'd decided to take his chance.

He caught something out of the corner of his eye. Lara hurried around the corner. He was just about to shout hello, when one minute she was on her feet, and the next she was on the ground with an uncomfortable thud.

"Lara!" He ran down the rest of the street, skidding a little as he finally reached her.

She stared up at the dark sky, looking completely stunned. She blinked and didn't say a word.

Ben dropped down onto his knees and moved closer, gently touching her shoulder. "Lara, are you okay? Have you hurt anything?"

After a few seconds, she gave a shudder as if the shock was finally leaving her. Her face screwed up. "Yeough," she said as she moved her body a little, squirming on the ice-covered street.

"Can you move your fingers, your toes? Do you need me to call an ambulance?" Panic was gripping him. Her fall had been pretty spectacular. Her legs had shot clean into the air before she'd hurtled back to the ground.

She shook her head. "No, no, I don't need an ambulance. Just give me a sec."

Pushing herself up onto one elbow, she let out a little yelp.

"Do you think you might have broken something?"

He watched as she rotated her ankles, then wiggled her fingers. "No, no, nothing's broken."

It was as if she'd just realized who he was. "The only thing I've hurt is my pride." She gave a rueful smile. "I think I left it back on the street somewhere."

"Here, let me help you." Before she had a chance to object, Ben slid his arms under her and picked her up, keeping her in his arms as he walked slowly and steadily down the street.

She gave a little yelp, "What are you doing? Put me down!"

He shook his head. "Watch out," he said as he kept his eyes on the restaurant door just ahead. "I'm concentrating completely on not slipping on this street. Believe me, you don't want me to land on top of you."

She stopped squiggling, fearful of landing on the rock-hard ice again. Her butt was sore enough already. When they reached the restaurant door, Ben gently lowered her to the ground and pushed the door open.

She tugged her coat back down and took a few breaths, trying to collect herself. "Thank you," she managed before one of the staff from the radio station almost jumped on top of them.

"There you are! What kept you? Come, come, we've set up a table for you both over here. The interviewer is waiting, and the photographer will be here in a few minutes. He's just parking his car."

The owner of Giuseppe's moved over, ignoring the pushy radio staff and beaming at Ben and Lara. "Welcome to Giuseppe's. Can I take your coats?" He shot the radio staffer a look. "Let me get my guests settled."

Ben was pleased. They hadn't even had a chance to catch their breath. He helped Lara slip off her thick wool coat. It was heavy, but hopefully had given her a bit of protection when she fell.

The door chimed behind them as the photographer came in, immediately bending down to talk to the interviewer.

Ben and Lara sat down at a booth near the back of the restaurant. The waiter gave them menus, listed all the specials, and the wines to match. He purposely positioned himself in front of the radio staff, giving Ben and Lara his full attention. "I want everyone who comes to Giuseppe's to enjoy their food," he said glancing over his shoulder, "Uninterrupted." He leaned forward. "How would you like to do this? Appetizers first, interview, and then your main courses once everyone has left?"

Lara gave Ben an amused smile and nodded her head a little. "Sounds good," he said.

He glanced at the menu. "So, are you going with your gut, or do you want to try one of the specials?"

She shook her head. "My heart lies with the pork-and-parmesan ravioli." Her eyes ran down the rest of the menu. "I'll have the salad to start, and a glass of Pinot Grigio, please."

Ben gave a smile. "I'll have the same, but with a glass of Pinot Noir."

The waiter disappeared for a few moments and Lara adjusted herself in the booth.

"Sore?"

It was the first chance he'd really gotten to look at her. She was wearing red. It suited her, complimenting her dark hair and eyes. He tried not to stare at the deep V in the front or the thin gold necklace around her neck.

She pulled a face. "A little. Bet I'll have some bruises tomorrow." She lifted a finger to stop him speaking. "And no, I won't be showing them to anyone."

"Where's the fun in that?" he teased, then shook his

head. "Seriously, if you don't feel up to this interview and dinner tonight, just let me know. We can rearrange."

She shook her head. "No, we're here now. I don't want them to harass me at work. We agreed to be part of the Christmas contest. If we want a chance to win the prize, I guess we need to play by the rules."

There was something in the way that she said those words that made him tilt his head. "You mean, you don't normally play by the rules?"

She didn't get a chance to answer before there was a voice at their side. "Hey, save the good stuff for the interview." A hand was stretched out toward Lara. "Lesley Slater, *Scandal and Home* magazine. Dave, come over here and snap some pictures."

Lara's eyes locked with Ben's. She was obviously just as surprised by the magazine name as he was. It was one of the best selling magazines, but was packed with scurrilous stories every week—usually not complimentary. Ben made a quick mental note. *In the future, do not agree to anything the radio station suggests without getting some more details first.*

The waiter appeared, tutting loudly with two glasses of wine.

"Perfect," Dave said. "Let's get a picture of you toasting each other."

Ben let out a groan. He turned his head away from the camera and kept his voice low. "Let's just give them what they want, then maybe we can get some peace."

Lara pressed her very red lips together. Had he really just noticed that?

"Sure," she murmured, her voice just as low.

She held up her wine glass and invited Dave to come closer, and they posed for picture after picture.

Ben was starting to get antsy, "You've got the patience of a saint," he muttered to Lara as Lesley shot interview questions all through their salads.

She looked up at him in surprise. "I've learned," she said. "I often help out at my grandmother's place. So many of her friends get forgetful or agitated—my grandmother, too. I've learned to take a breath and be patient. You must get that at the school, too," she said, her dark eyes fixed on his. "Are you telling me the teenagers don't occasionally try your patience?"

He could feel himself light up. "Every single day. But they also give me joy. We were lucky. Social media was just starting out when we were teenagers. Nowadays, you can have a thousand people commenting on your appearance or shouting at you within minutes."

She nodded thoughtfully. "Of course. I've had a million friend requests from people I don't know in the last few days. Have you?"

"Not quite a million." He felt himself bristle a little at the thought of random strangers seeking Lara out online. He would bet that most were male.

She laughed and waved her hand. "No, just a figure of

speech. Not really a million. But it felt like that the other night when I got home." She raised her eyebrows. "Some attached messages."

"Did you read them?"

She shook her head. "Of course I didn't." She paused. "Have you?"

"No. But I've had a lot of messages about work, too. Some are just a waste of time, but some of them are genuine. You could say that business is booming."

"That must be nice."

"It is, but it's a bit overwhelming. There's just me. I don't like to let people down, and I don't like to say no."

"Maybe you need an assistant?"

He shrugged. "Maybe I do, but I just don't have time."

He looked up and realized that Lesley was scribbling frantically. He glanced over at the waiter, who seemed to read the situation and come over, clapping his hands.

"Right guys, I think that's long enough. I have other guests in the restaurant that don't want to be disturbed. Time's up."

Lara shot him a grateful look. It was clear she'd had enough. Ben had, too.

Dave and Lesley didn't look particularly happy about being handed their coats and swiftly ushered out the door. The waiter appeared back a few minutes later with two plates of steaming ravioli and topped off their wine glasses.

"Now" he said with a flourish. "Enjoy!"

Ben and Lara let out mutual sighs of relief and relaxed back into their seats in the booth.

The aroma from the ravioli was exquisite, but the taste was even better.

Both of them sipped at their wine. Now the photographer and interviewer were gone, the Italian restaurant had the ambience it should. Dim lights, candles flickering on the tables, low, quiet conversations between guests, and soft music in the background.

"Worried about tomorrow night?"

Lara's head shot up. "No. Why would I be?"

It looked like he'd hit a nerve. "No reason."

She shifted in her chair, then put down her fork. "I was hoping for a bit of muscle," she admitted. "But it looks like it will be one of the girls helping me."

He gave a nod. "If you have a problem, I could help," he offered.

Her eyes widened. "That would be cheating."

He shrugged. "Not really. You'll build the snowman. If you need hand in lifting it, I'm sure Rudy and I can help you."

Something flitted across her eyes. She was actually considering the offer. But then she picked up her fork again and shook her head. "No. I think the listeners wouldn't think it was fair." She gave a smile. "I don't want them all to vote against me."

"Okay." He paused for a second, "Are you enjoying the

contest?"

There were a few seconds of silence as she clearly contemplated her answer. "I didn't mind the questions or the tasks. I'm not sure I like the constant intrusion."

He nodded. "I know what you mean."

"But it's good for your business." She let out a short laugh. "By the end of the contest, you won't need the prize money. You'll be able to buy a new gym floor with all your profits."

He sat back in the booth. "Are you asking me to give up?"

"What? No." She looked genuinely surprised.

"It sounded like it." He set his fork down, annoyed. His plan had been to enjoy this dinner. To get to know Lara a little better, without the glare of the radio station around them.

"Listen, about the interview."

"Yes?" His words came out sharper than he meant them to.

"You know that particular magazine is notorious for twisting words?"

"Yeah, I do know. But the radio station obviously thinks it will be good publicity. Why would they set us up otherwise?"

She shifted again and put her hand to her back. "I know, but I just don't really trust them. I'd hate them to misinterpret anything we've said."

"I guess we'll just have to wait and see."

"Yes, we do." They'd both set their cutlery down. A silence seemed to envelope them. After a rocky start, Ben had thought the evening might go well. He couldn't pretend that he wasn't intrigued by Lara.

But she just seemed so focused on the contest. So intent on winning. It made him doubt himself. On a few occasions, he'd wondered if there might be something in the air between them. But now, it seemed like it had all been his imagination.

She arched her back a little again.

"Are you sore?"

She gave a sorry nod.

"Why don't we call it a night then? You should go home and rest. Take some painkillers."

She kept nodding as she stood up and Ben gestured for their coats and the bill. The waiter approached a moment later, their coats over his arm. "The bill has been paid," he waved his hand. "The radio station paid in advance, and they've arranged a cab for you both."

"Oh," they said in unison, their eyes meeting.

"I guess that's a good idea," Lara said, with a half-smile. "It's icy out there."

Disappointment flooded through Ben like a slow, ebbing tide. He hadn't realized quite how much he'd been looking forward to tonight. And now? He couldn't even offer to walk her home so they could chat some more.

Lara was feisty. She was interesting. And he wanted to get to know her better.

But she clearly didn't.

He waited until the first cab arrived, and then opened the door for her. "Goodnight."

She paused for a second as if she were going to say something else, but then, "Goodnight," came from her lips with a reluctance he couldn't pretend not to notice.

Ben closed the door, then watched the cab sweep down the street until the taillights faded. He stuck in his hands in his pockets. "Cancel the other cab," he told the waiter. "It seems like I need the cold air."

He started down the street. The Christmas decorations in the shop windows seemed a little jaded now. His breath formed smoky clouds in front of him in the icy air and the temperature nipped at his skin as his feet crunched on the ground beneath him.

Tomorrow was another day. He'd have to plan for the snowman. And no matter how Lara looked at him, he intended on having a plan good enough to win it.

There was no time like the present. He pulled his phone from his pocket and started searching 'best ever snowmen' on the walk home.

He scrolled through pages of pictures before he paused at one in particular. "Got it," he said as a smile appeared across his face.

Chapter Eight

B EN TURNED OVER as his phone rang. As he went to grab it, his heart skipped a beat. It was early. Who would be calling this time in the morning? It was barely past six.

"Hello?"

"Ben, great, I've caught you. It's Abe. Abe Rogers."

Ben sat upright, his forehead wrinkling. Abe was a friend from years ago—one Ben had played pro-baseball with. Except Abe had made it all the way to the major league.

"Nice to hear from you. What can I do for you, Abe?"

They'd never been the best of friends, but the guy had been amiable and friendly on every occasion they'd met. This call was definitely unusual.

"It's what I can do for you. I heard you're taking part in a competition tonight. I'm phoning to offer my services to help you win the vote."

"What?" Ben's brain couldn't quite catch up. Abe wanted to come and help him build a snowman? That was just plain crazy.

"Yeah, I'm in your neck of the woods. My publicist heard we used to play together and thought it could be fun."

Ben's stomach curled. Abe's publicist. Of course. He took a deep breath. "That's really kind of you, Abe, and I appreciate the call and the offer. But I'm doing this for the high school kids, and one of them has already been chosen to help me tonight. If I put him off, the kid will be devastated—and I can't do that to him."

"Wouldn't he want to meet a major league baseball player?" Abe sounded surprised and a little indignant.

Ben gave a nervous laugh. "I'm sure he would. But I'm also sure he'd fight you to the death for his spot on the snowman team."

"Oh...okay. Sure." Ben could hear murmuring in the background. A few seconds later, Abe was back on the line. "Right, okay then."

It was clear the call was over, but a thought came into Ben's mind.

"Abe? Would you consider something else?"

"What?" The answer came warily.

"How about helping the competition?" Ben wasn't quite sure where the idea came from. Maybe it was the look on Lara's face last night when she'd said she couldn't really find anyone strong enough to help her.

"Are you serious?"

"Sure." Ben nodded his head even though Abe couldn't see him. "She had a bit of a fall last night and got injured. She would probably appreciate the help tonight."

"Oh, yeah, I saw that. Looked like she had some help,

though."

Ben straightened. "What do you mean?"

"You've still got it—haven't you? Anyhow..." There were a few murmurs again before Abe said, "Help your competition? Sure, no problem. See you tonight, Ben."

The phone cut off before Ben had a chance to say anything else, but his brain was already in overdrive.

He pulled up a search engine on his phone and typed in his name. The page filled with hits from last night and this morning.

He froze. A close-up shot of him, walking along with Lara in his arms. It must have been taken last night.

The photographer had zoomed right in on them. And the expressions on both of their faces made Ben jerk back from the screen. They were looking at each other and smiling, maybe even laughing a little. But it was the look in both of their eyes that took him by surprise.

Ben hadn't known he'd looked at Lara like that.

He hadn't known that *she'd* looked at him like that.

It took his breath away and he gulped.

His eyes scanned the page. He didn't need to read the text. He could see the headline. *Contest competitors secretly dating!*

He clenched his hand around his phone as he scrolled down and saw some of the comments. Four hundred and fifty-six. This picture had been published a few hours ago...and there were Four hundred and fifty-six comments *already?*

He groaned. He could only imagine the ribbing he would get from the kids today. And from the look of that picture, he deserved it.

But what would Lara think? His stomach twisted uncomfortably. If he was shocked by the picture, he imagined she would be, too.

He could almost hear her workmates already. Ben let out a sigh. For the first time in forever, he was glad he worked alone.

But as his phone started to light up with texts, he knew his peace for the day was about to be shattered.

◈

SHE HAD A nicely emerging purple-and-yellow bruise on her backside that she could just about see in the bathroom mirror if she stood on her tiptoes.

Lara shook her head as she pulled a black sweater over her head, to match her red jeggings and sturdy black boots. She was wearing clothes today that would match her footwear. She had no intention of a repeat of last night—in more ways than one.

What on earth had been wrong with her? She hadn't meant to sound snappy with Ben. It had just sounded as if things were going so well for him that he might not even need the contest. She, on the other hand, would never have a chance of finding or earning that money in any other way. Not unless she won the lottery. And the chances of that were millions to one.

Her phone started ringing and she pulled her sweater back down and grabbed for it, not even looking to see the name.

"Lara Cottridge."

"Well hi Lara Cottridge, this is Abe Rogers from the Vermont Bulls."

She opened her mouth to speak, but nothing came out. The Vermont Bulls? The baseball team? The image of a handsome tall, dark-skinned man swam in front of her eyes.

"Lara, are you still there?"

She caught her breath. "Yes, yes, I'm here. I'm sorry. You just surprised me."

"Well, that's good. Listen, I was phoning to offer you my services at the competition tonight."

She was dumfounded and found herself stuttering. "Wh-what do you mean?"

"For the snowman building competition. I gather you're looking for a bit of muscle. Well, here I am. Happy to help. I'm in the area tonight, and Ben told me you might need a hand." He let out a low laugh, "I kind of like the idea of beating a former teammate."

Lara took a deep breath. "You want to help me build a snowman?" She still couldn't quite believe this call.

"You want me to break into song to prove it?"

"What? No. Well, maybe. That could work tonight." A smile started to spread across her face. "If you could help, that would be great."

"Well great. It's at seven, isn't it? I'll be there before then."

A million thoughts flooded her brain. What would they build? What about a theme? But before she got a chance to say another word, Abe cut her off. "See you tonight then."

She stared at the phone in her hand. Not quite believing what had just happened. Was she dreaming? Maybe she hadn't even woken up yet?

But as she tugged the brush through her hair, her phone started to go crazy. She hadn't even looked at it properly this morning. There was consistent noise and it took her a few seconds to realize it was a few hundred messages download-ing at once, sounding like a symphony orchestra. Some voice messages, some texts. Had people heard about Abe already? How could that even be possible?

As she grabbed her coat and gloves, a thought flew into her head. *Ben.* Abe had phoned her because of Ben. She stopped for a second. She'd mentioned last night she was struggling for help with the snowman. He'd offered her help, which she knew the contest wouldn't have allowed—but after her snappiness last night, she was surprised the offer still stood.

Better even. He'd roped in a friend. A famous friend who would likely have a fan base that would make her votes rise higher.

Why would Ben do that for her? Wouldn't it have made more sense for him to bring his former teammate on board to generate the publicity for himself?

Her hand froze on the door handle. She'd have to thank him. She'd have to get his number and phone him. Her grandmother had always emphasized the importance of good manners, and Lara couldn't let her down now.

She ignored the messages on her phone, assuming they were all to do with Abe, as she made her way to work. But as soon as she stepped into the office, the buzzing conversation that was happening in the far corner stopped.

All eyes turned to her, and her skin prickled.

She peeled off her coat. "I take it you've all heard," she said as she put a big smile on her face, ready for all the questions about Abe.

Rae pulled a face. "Isn't that kind of cheating?"

Lara dumped her bag on her desk. She hadn't expected that kind of question. "Well, no, not really. He offered to help. I need the muscle. You all know that no one from the hospital was available."

Confusion swept across the faces around her.

But she kept talking. "And think of the votes he'll pull in for me. This could work out really well."

"It's not real?"

"You did it to pull in votes?"

Lara shook her head. Something about this felt wrong.

The girls in the office were usually so supportive.

"Guys, what are you talking about?"

Rae lifted a copy of the local newspaper off her desk, thrusting it toward Lara. "This. Why, what are *you* talking about?"

Lara leaned forward, peering at the black-and-white picture on the front page, letting out a gasp as she realized what she was looking at.

She grabbed the paper from Rae's hands "Where on earth did this come from?"

It didn't matter. The name of the paper and the date was clearly on the front, but none of this seemed real.

"The store," Rae said blankly.

All of a sudden all the eyes on her seemed really invasive. "Who took this? When did this happen?" It was like a veil fell from her eyes as the pieces slotted into place. "That photographer. Last night. The rat bag. How dare he take a picture of me without my permission?"

Her mouth was running away from her. But her brain was stuck on the picture in front of her. Ben was grinning, holding her in his arms. She had one arm around his shoulder and her other hand resting against his chest. Almost as if they did that every day. And she was smiling, too. Lara couldn't even remember that happening last night. The guy must have taken a million photos to capture this second in time.

And that made her mad. Because it felt intensely private.

The look in Ben's eyes as he held her close made her mouth dry. But the look she was giving him back made her heart twist in her chest. It was like she was telling the whole world exactly how she felt about him. Something that *she* hadn't even realized.

She looked back up and the faces were all staring at her.

"What?" she snapped, then flinched. What was wrong with her? That was two days in a row she'd been snappy. She was never like this.

"So, is something going on between you and Ben?"

"When did that happen?"

"Have you kissed him?"

The questions seemed to come from all angles. Lara tried to answer them all. "No, nothing's going on. I fell in the street, and he picked me up. Of course I haven't kissed him. After last night, I didn't even think he'd want to talk to me this morning, then Abe Rogers phoned and—"

"Abe Rogers phoned you?"

Rae's voice was louder than the rest.

Lara sighed. Too much was happening at once. "Yeah, that's what I thought you were all talking about when I came in."

"What did he call you for?"

"To offer to be my partner for the snowman competition. He heard I needed some muscle."

"How did he hear that?"

Lara waved her hand. "Ben must have told him. I'd mentioned it last night, and—"

"Wait." Rae put up her hand. "Rewind. Why did you think Ben wouldn't be talking to you? What did you do last night?"

It was all getting too much. Lara sagged down into her seat and put her head in her hands. "Oh, I snapped at him. I might even have hinted he should drop out of the competition."

"You did what?" The indignation in her friend's voice was clear.

Lara leaned back in her chair and threw up her hands. "Whose side are you on?"

Rae folded her arms. "Right now, Ben's."

Lara's voice wobbled. "Guys. This is hard enough. I need you all to back me."

"Then act like the kind of girl we want to back. What's gotten into you?"

Lara sucked in a deep breath. "I don't know." She shook her head, "Every time I visit my grandmother all I can see is how much that money could do to make life a little bit nicer for them all. A little bit more sparkly. Shouldn't they get that? And they all know I'm trying. But what if it's not enough? What if I try my best, and it's still not good enough?"

The tension in the room seemed to evaporate around her. Rae sunk into the chair at her side. "Of course you're good enough. This is just a lousy competition, Lara. It was supposed to be a bit of fun. We were just talking that all of us have noticed more people in town. The publicity is definitely bringing in business."

Lara nodded. "And that's what Ben said. He's getting more emails about business than he can deal with. The publicity has really given his business a boost."

"So you hinted he should drop out?"

She pulled a face. "I might have."

The expression on Rae's face changed and folded her arms across her chest. "So, you hinted he should drop out. And in return, he gets you some kind of baseball superstar to build a snowman with you tonight?"

Lara put her head down on the desk. "Don't. I feel bad enough already. Don't remind me that he's clearly a much better person than me."

Abby picked up the paper and folded it, so only the photo was visible. "Oh, it's not he's a better person. This tells us all we need to know. The guy is smitten."

The rest of the girls let out a whoop. Lara's head shot back up. "He is not."

Abby smiled, "They say a picture tells a thousand words. What do you think girls, what's that picture telling you?" She held it up and turned around.

Rae nudged her. "I don't think he's the only one that's smitten," she said in a low voice.

Lara felt her cheeks flame. "Rae!" She batted her with her palm. "Stop it."

Rae shrugged. "Just calling like I see it." She tilted her head to the side as Abby lay the paper back down on the desk. Rae pulled it toward her. "Thing is Lara. With one guy looking at you like that, and another baseball hottie coming to help tonight, which one will you choose?"

Lara's mouth fell open. "What do you mean? Abe Roger is only coming up to help out. His team must have asked him to do it or something."

Abby leaned her head on one hand. "Doesn't mean you can't make Guy Number One a little jealous."

"Why would I do that?"

"Oh honey. You're telling us that he's not smitten. We're telling you that he is. Simple way to find out. Why don't you bat those long eyelashes a little at Abe Roger tonight, and see how Mr. Winters likes it?"

Lara was stunned. This was the last thing she expected to hear. "No," was the word that immediately shot to her lips.

She could swear her heart was curling somewhere inside her chest. Because she wouldn't do that. She would never do that. Flirt to make another man jealous.

Abby moved over and put hip on the edge of the desk, giving Lara a skeptical glance. "It's okay, Rae," she said. "There's nothing going on between them, and Lara wouldn't flirt unnecessarily with another handsome guy. Why would she? It's not like she needs the publicity to win the votes." Abby's eyebrows flickered upward for a second. "But it might be helpful."

The words settled uncomfortably in the pit of Lara's stomach. None of this made her happy. Not the photo in the newspaper. Not the thought of how that made her feel. And definitely not the thought of using the competition to make Ben jealous.

She sighed. Would he even care? Would he even be jealous?

"No," she said again. "I signed up to take part in this competition fair and square. I'm not going to do something underhand to try and win—even if that's flirting."

Abby made an exasperated sound as she stood, "Well, move over then honey, because there's a queue of women waiting to replace you."

And she sashayed out of the office leaving Lara dumbstruck.

Chapter Nine

ABE WAS EVERY bit the charmer that Ben remembered. All bright eyes and flashing teeth. Ben also recognized a few of the staff from the Vermont Bulls, obviously there to make sure their star ticked all the boxes for the publicity they wanted.

Even Marty at the radio station seemed a little awed by Abe's presence. He kept stumbling over his words and dropping things into the conversation, "Remember when I interviewed you…"

Ben tried not to smile. It was clear that Abe didn't remember a single thing about it, but he was far too polished to say that. Rudy, on the other hand, just stood open-mouthed, hanging on Abe's every word, and Ben wasn't entirely sure that he liked that.

Abe was dressed in his usual designer gear—all of which was completely appropriate for the weather and the task ahead—and all of which was likely sponsored by the clothing companies. That was how these things usually worked.

"Those boots cost four hundred dollars," Rudy whispered as he looked at Abe's feet. His eyes widened as he caught a glimpse of a symbol on the jacket. "And isn't that jacket over a thousand bucks?"

"I have no idea," Ben said truthfully. "But, at the end of the day, it's just a jacket."

This was a battle he couldn't win, and he knew it. And he understood, because he'd been sucked into that world at one point, too. At least Abe was a decent human being. He would never be rude or talk down to people. He was confident enough that Rudy's dreams of meeting a sports hero weren't about to be shattered.

Abe saw him and gave a yell and a big wave. "Ben!"

Ben walked over in long strides and enveloped him in a bear hug. "How you doing?"

Ben smiled as the publicity people, both from the radio and from the Vermont Bulls, all simultaneously chattered, "Get their reunion on camera!"

He played along, shaking hands and chatting away to Abe. "Sorry about earlier, but I already had my right-hand man. This is Rudy." He slung an arm around Rudy's shoulder and pulled the boy closer so he could meet Abe.

Rudy was wide-eyed and started firing off a thousand questions. Abe answered good-naturedly while posing for a selfie with him.

Ben looked around. "Have you met Lara yet?"

Abe shrugged. "Only briefly. They pulled her into makeup and wardrobe before she'd barely had a chance to say hello." He side-eyed Ben. "She seems...very nice." It was as if he'd chosen those words carefully. Then he gave Ben a little nudge, leaning over to whisper in his ear. "I saw the press picture. Is there something going on between you two?"

Rudy caught the end of the conversation and laughed out loud, slapping Ben on the arm. "He wishes. We've been teasing him about it all afternoon."

Ben cast a glance at the door Lara would emerge from. He didn't really want to be caught discussing her. He shook his head. "No, no, nothing going on. We're just friendly rivals."

Abe looked him square in the eye, but he didn't say anything out loud. He didn't believe a single word of it. A warm feeling spread across Ben's stomach. He didn't mind Abe thinking there might be something going on between him and Lara. He wasn't sure if Abe had a partner at present, but at least now he would consider Lara off limits.

Abe put his hand on Rudy's shoulder. "Wanna help me warm up? Throw some balls before our contest?"

Rudy jumped for joy. "Sure."

Abe put an arm around Rudy's shoulder and they walked out into the snow where lights had been set up for the snowman contest. Abe smiled at Ben over his shoulder, and Ben nodded. The publicity people would love this. He imagined that they'd probably suggested Abe warm up with Ben. But, for Ben, that would have been a bit embarrassing. The super star and the could-have-been? He was happy with his life. He didn't want people to think he was stuck in the past. Abe had the good grace to understand that.

Lara emerged from the other room, wrinkling her nose. She walked over and stood next to Ben, staring out at Abe and Rudy. "Thank you," she said quietly.

"For what?"

She gestured with her hand. "For that. For Abe. For suggesting he help me. It'll create some great publicity for Briarhill Falls."

Ben resisted the temptation to press his lips together as all the 'I regretted it' thoughts flew through his mind. "People like Abe," he said steadily, "could bring you in a lot of votes."

"Why didn't you work with him yourself?"

Ben could give a multitude of answers. But he stuck with the one that had been his first response. "I'd promised Rudy. This is about the kids. Rudy was so excited that he might be on the live stream, and he would have been devastated if I told him he'd been replaced. I just couldn't do it."

She reached over and touched his arm, giving a squeeze. "That's nice. You're a good person, Ben Winters."

She held his gaze. Any words he might have said left his brain completely. For a few moments, it was just the two of them standing in the snow, their breath clouding the air around them.

Her face broke into a wide grin. "You're staring," she said, then leaned a little closer. "It's okay. I know I'm orange.

They put too much makeup on me. Apparently, my own makeup isn't good enough anymore. And this coat?" She tugged at the bright green wool coat. "It's very nice, but it's a bit snug and definitely out my price zone." She looked down, then glanced back up at him with a wrinkle across her brow. "Do I look like a Christmas tree? It's okay, you can tell me."

He laughed out loud. "You look very nice." He bent down to whisper in her ear, "But when they come at you with the hat that's secretly a giant star, run!"

She laughed as Marty hurried over. "Well, if it isn't our delectable couple…is love in the air?"

He looked so pleased with himself.

"No," they said simultaneously. Ben wondered if he should be offended by how quickly the words flew out of their mouths.

"Really?" Marty's eyebrows comically arched. "Well, we had over two thousand enquiries about the two of you at the radio station tonight, so I expect the viewing and listening figures to skyrocket." He clapped his hands together and wandered off, shouting, "Five minutes," over his shoulder.

Lara looked a bit panicked. "But it was just one photograph. Nothing else. There wasn't anything else to see. It's silly really." He watched, a little fascinated, as it was clear she couldn't stop talking. "I mean, you only carried me a few hundred yards. And anyone could see from that picture that it was a temporary arrangement. It wasn't like we were kissing or caught in some kind of compromising position. I think people just see what they want to see. Maybe the radio station planned all this? Do you think they could be behind the photo?"

Was she trying to convince *him* there was nothing between them—or herself? That was the first thought that landed in Ben's head. He couldn't help but smile as he answered. "It's clear they're behind it. Don't you remember Dave the photographer coming in behind us? He must have snapped us from the street outside."

"Of course." Her hand flew to her mouth, then her hands went to her hips. "I feel manipulated, and I don't like it." She tilted her chin upward as if she were readying herself to start a fight.

He put a hand on her shoulder. "Save it for later. We have a snowman to build."

He finished speaking just as Marty launched into his opening spiel and shouted them both over, introducing them and their snow-building partners to the listeners on radio and the viewers on the stream.

He'd brought a small bag with him with a hat, scarf, carrot, and pipe for their snowman, but now he noticed Lara seemed to have a whole lot more.

Maybe he should have planned a little better—but how hard could building a snowman be? Seemed he was just about to find out.

SOMETHING HAD FLICKERED inside when she'd been speaking to Ben. There had just been some kind of buzz between them. She knew her mouth had run away with her at one point, but she just couldn't stop it. Listing all the reasons that it was ridiculous people thought they were together while trying to be indignant about it…when the truth was, the look they shared in that photograph had haunted her all day.

She'd had to retype a letter three times before finally getting it right, all because she couldn't concentrate on her work.

She'd put the newspaper in a drawer, but had then spent the day willing herself not to open it and stare at the look in her eyes, and the look in his.

Thankfully, for at least five minutes, Abe Rogers had managed to distract her. He was charm personified. She wasn't entirely convinced by his enthusiasm. From the way he was surrounded by staff from the Vermont Bulls, it was clear they had their own agenda. But as long as he could follow instructions and lift the snowballs on top of one another—she was happy.

She'd positioned herself at his far side, happy to let him take the lead for the interview with Marty, telling people why he was here, and talking a little about himself. She tugged at her gloves, hoping the wetness wouldn't get through. They were supposed to be waterproof, but as a long-time resident of Vermont, she'd heard all those claims before.

She stared at the brand and blinked. These were designer gloves—just like the coat. She'd bet they wouldn't keep the cold, or the wet, out for more than five minutes. But apparently the radio station had made a temporary deal with some company for the next few trials. It could be designer clothes all the way.

She pulled out the piece of folded paper she'd tucked into the pocket. Marty was just about finished talking.

"So, folks, are you ready? Are you steady? Then go!"

They were in a central piece of ground in the middle of the town square that was covered with a thick layer of snow and illuminated by four bright lights set up in the corners of the ground.

It was a bit like being under a spotlight.

Abe moved over next to her, beaming. "Right, team, are we ready?"

She gave a nod and unfolded the paper. "Here's our plan." For a few seconds, his eyes widened, then, if it were possible, his grin got even wider. He nodded and looked down at her, "I like you. You're a clever girl. We're going to rock this."

He punched the air, then shouted over to Ben and Rudy. "Hey, friend, watch us and weep. You're going down!"

Lara burst out laughing at the theatrics. The crowd filling the streets to watch them whooped and clapped.

She and Abe had a low conversation about where to start before they started rolling their first snowball.

Rudy was working at the opposite side of the green, almost in parallel. His eyes lit up as he saw Abe start to roll, and he tried to match him and keep pace.

Ben moved to help, then stopped. It was clear he could see the fun and admiration in Rudy's gaze while watching Abe. He gave an almost unnoticeable nod of his head as he made sure the attention was clearly on Rudy.

Even though it was bitter cold, a warm feeling spread through Lara. He had a good heart. He put the interests of these kids first. Always encouraging, always thinking about them.

A few of the workers from her grandmother's sheltered housing complex had bundled up some of their clients in some wheelchairs and brought them down. Her grandmother had been too sick. She'd spent last night with a temperature, and the doctor was scheduled to see her tomorrow.

Lara started gathering snow for the next snowball, wishing that she were there. Abe returned to her side, ready to take over, and she sighed.

"What's wrong?"

She shook her head. "Nothing. You're doing great." She looked to where he'd put the first snowball, directly in the spot she'd marked for him. "I've made snowmen here since I was a kid. I'm just hoping it snows again tonight so that the kids get to do it all again tomorrow."

Abe's face lost its permanent grin. "Bringing back memories for you?"

She nodded, suddenly unable to find the words. She just really wished her grandmother could have been there to see this.

Abe looked over to the other side of the green, where Ben and Rudy were working together. He looked back at her thoughtfully, "Maybe it's time to make some new memories?"

He didn't say anything else. Just let those words sit for a few moments, while Marty started commenting in the background about what was going on.

The staff member doing the live stream came over, shining yet another light on their faces, that jerked them back to reality. "Give the viewers a wave," she shouted.

Abe moved straight back into professional mode, playing for the camera, and Lara was grateful. It meant she could fade into the background a little.

Abe finished rolling the second snowball and lifted it easily onto the first. Both were bigger than she could have managed on her own. She just hoped he'd manage to lift the final one.

On the other side, Ben and Rudy were lifting their second snowball up together, teetering a little with the motion.

She smiled. They were going for a traditional build. The

really big snowball at the bottom, and the smaller head-sized one on the top. It was still striking. Now the head on their snowman was at least as tall as she was.

Ben gave her a quizzical stare as he looked at her two identically sized snowballs, as Abe started rolling the third she'd started.

He hadn't worked out what she was doing yet and that made her happy. He saw her watching, and shouted over good-naturedly. "I thought you wanted big? Abe, is that the best you can do?"

The two of them started jibing back and forward, joking with each other. The crowd loved it. Marty was sweating, running back and forth between them both. The radio listeners would be able to hear everything, as two studio hands were positioned with microphones, and the crowd was thoroughly entertained. One of the team ran over and whispered something in Marty's ear and he looked like he could take off like a firework.

"Guess what, folks, we've just heard that tonight's show has the highest number of listeners ever for a KNWZ show! Isn't that just spectacular?" He moved over next to them again and looked at his watch. "Ten minutes, folks. That's all the time you have left. Keep working!"

Abe gave her a nod. "Ready?"

She grinned and watched as he lifted the third and last snowball on top. The bag she'd brought with her was sitting at the side, and she grabbed it. Two long bendy sticks were protruding from the top.

She looked sideways. Ben and Rudy were sticking a traditional hat and scarf on their snowman. It was good. It was sturdy.

Lara emptied her bag, lifted three bits of coal and stuck them down the middle ball. She stuck the large bendy twigs into the side of the second ball but instead of pointing them upward and outwards, she bent them back and stuck them into the ground.

Then, she got down on her hands and knees, wrapping the scarf between the bottom and middle ball, putting the carrot into the bottom ball, two more pieces of coal underneath, and then a very small bendy twig, curved into a upside-down smile above the carrot.

She could hear the people murmuring all around her. Then, after a few seconds, they all tilted their heads to the side. It was fun to watch as recognition dawned on all their faces, Ben and Rudy's included.

Marty stood to the side and let out a giant yell. "How clever! Folks, we have an upside-down snowman! He's sooooo cute!"

The people around them started to applaud. One of the staff ran forward with a camera to snap both snowmen, giving a thumbs-up to Marty.

"Our two snowmen will be on our website in just a matter of seconds. You'll be able to vote for which one you like the best. But do it quickly—you only have an hour before we announce the winner."

Lara's stomach clenched. An hour? That was new. They hadn't warned them about that. She'd kind of hoped it would run for twenty-four hours like the last vote so she'd have time to spread the word throughout the hospital.

Abe sensed her flash of worry. He sauntered over, putting his arm around her shoulders. "Don't worry, girl. We got this. You nailed it." He laughed as he tilted his own head to look at their snowman.

She wished she could be as casually confident as he was. Her skin prickled, and she looked over. Ben watched her, his gaze fixed on her.

In an instant, she could hear Abby's voice from earlier. Teasing Lara about the way they'd looked at each other and advising her to flirt with Abe. That just wasn't in her nature. She wouldn't do that. And even though Abe had put his arm around her shoulders, it was clear he would do that with anyone.

"Team Lara," he yelled at the crowd as he punched the air.

"Team Winters," Rudy shouted back instantly.

The crowd started laughing, and Ben's gaze broke with hers as he turned his attention to Rudy. Ben could play to the crowd just as much as Abe could, and they teased each other, jibing and joking for the next few minutes. Marty was in his element, keeping them both on air.

He included Rudy and some of the other high school

kids who were there watching. It was turning into a party.

Ben moved over next to her. Folding his arms, he tilted his head once again. "I like it," he said. "You did good."

She smiled, staring at her snowman. "I did, didn't I?"

"Wish I'd thought of it," Ben admitted.

"I just wanted to try something different. Something that might catch the eye, but not be overcomplicated."

Ben looked back at Rudy, who was now laughing and joking with Abe. He took a slow breath. "I just hope Rudy won't be disappointed when we don't get many votes."

Lara pulled back. "You'll get votes. Of course you will."

Ben waved a hand. "What, when you have Abe Rogers, superhero, on your team *and* an upside-down snowman?" He smiled and shook his head. "It's fine—I know when I'm beat."

Lara glanced over her shoulder to a spot of snow that had been left unmarked.

Ben shot her a curious look. "What? What is it?"

She shook her head quickly. "Nothing."

But it was clear she'd sparked his attention. "It's not nothing. Tell me."

She bit her lip, unsure if she should really say what was on her mind. She looked back over at Marty, who was still interviewing Rudy and Abe.

"It's just…whenever I built a snowman here when I was a kid, when we were finished, there was always a final step."

She turned her face to Ben's.

"Snow angels," they said in unison.

Her eyes widened in surprise, and so did his.

"What? You did that, too?"

She held out her hands. "Didn't everyone? You can't build a snowman and not finish with a snow angel. Every Christmas holiday I spent with my parents and grandma here, that was always the next step."

A determined look spread across his face, and he held out his gloved hand towards her. "Come on."

Her mouth opened. "We can't."

"Who says we can't? We've done the contest. We've built the snowman. Now, it's our time. Now, we get to do what we want."

There was a mischievous glint in his eye. "Are you chicken?"

That was all it took. She was halfway there already, but those final words were enough to give her the push she needed.

She reached out her hand and put it in his. With a quick glance over his shoulder, Ben pulled her over to the perfect, unmarked patch of snow.

The crowd was all gathered around the other side, watching the show.

Ben and Lara took a few tentative steps into the snow. They both turned around, so they were facing the faraway crowd.

Ben held out his arms, and Lara followed suit. They were

professionals. If you'd done snow angels often enough, it was easy to judge exactly where to stand in comparison to your neighbor.

"Ready?" His eyes were shining, the reflection from the snow brightening up his skin.

"Ready," she agreed, her arms trembling a little as she kept holding them out.

"Go," he yelled before falling backward.

She had half a second to pray that the snowfall was thick enough to cushion her fall before landing backward on the ground.

A *poof* of white snowflakes fluttered up around her before she started moving her legs and arms frantically, laughing.

It was the most she'd ever heard Ben laugh before, as snow got into every part of her. Down the neck of her coat, up her sleeves, and in the zipper of her boots.

For a few moments, it was just Lara and Ben, recreating past childhood memories, and reliving the sensations of a life long ago. And she liked it. She might have even loved it. She'd turned her head toward him, ignoring the snow soaking her hair and trying to find its way into her ear. He was laughing just as hard as she was.

It only took the rest of the people a few seconds to notice what they were doing. Marty let out a shriek, as he, Abe, and Rudy ran over, clapping and pointing at them.

The girl filming the live stream spun around to catch them on her web cam. For the first few seconds, she smiled, too, then her face dropped like a stone and she shouted to one of her colleagues.

Lara stopped waving her arms about, wondering what the problem was. The wet was starting to penetrate through to her back, so she pushed herself up, sitting straight.

A minute later, the wardrobe girl ran over, face frozen in horror.

"Lara," she exclaimed in shock, her hand outstretched. "The coat."

Oops. Lara looked down. She'd completely forgotten she was wearing the coat and the gloves. She stood up quickly and brushed off the coat, completely aware the back of it must be completely saturated. She tugged at it.

It still looked good. It was a coat. How much damage could snow and water do?

She pulled a rueful face. "Sorry."

The girl's face was pale. Had Lara gotten her into trouble?

As Marty turned around with the microphone, ready to speak to her, Lara felt herself go into self-recovery mode.

"I've had such a great time tonight—just reliving a few childhood moments there." She beamed at the girl live streaming. "But isn't my coat great? So warm. And I'm still dry as a bone!"

Ben shot her a look, knowing her back was completely soaked, but he moved alongside her. Marty didn't seem to hear what she'd said. He had other things on his mind.

"So, what about the rumors? The pictures?" He let out a loud, false laugh. "And you two creeping off into the corner—is there love in the air?"

Ben moved in smoothly. "We were just reminiscing about childhoods. We both used to build snowmen here. And we both used to make snow angels. But we never met. Weird, isn't it?"

He was looking at her now. As if he couldn't quite believe it himself.

Lara licked her lips. She hadn't really thought about it too much. "I guess our paths never really crossed." She looked back at Marty, "Ben was a few years older than me in high school. Then, he played baseball for a few years. I guess by the time he came back to Briarhill Falls, I'd left for college. Over the last few years, we've both been so busy. We just never came across each other."

"And now you have," Marty said, his voice laced with conspiracy. "It was almost like it was meant to be. Fate, even."

The words were left hanging in the air between them. Neither of them spoke. Then, as if someone up above was in charge of distraction techniques, large flakes of snow started falling around them.

Abe appeared next to them, shooting them a smile. "Here we have it, snow for the next round tomorrow." He gave Lara a little nod, and she knew he was referring to what she'd said earlier.

Ben took a step back, as if he'd noticed the glance. When he walked back over to Rudy, Lara felt her heart sink a little.

She'd felt a few moments of magic earlier, when it had been just the two of them and no one else had noticed what they were doing.

The crowd gathered around the two snowmen now, taking pictures and posing next to them. It was getting late, but lots of young kids were still up, enjoying all the fun that came along with the contest. Lara grabbed Abe's arm and took him over to meet her grandmother's friends, making sure he posed for pictures with them. The care staff seemed anxious to take their charges home. "Sorry we can't wait for the announcement," Lacey said to her, "but it's getting too cold, and we're sure you've won anyhow."

She reached over to squeeze Lara's hand. "You've done so well. I can't wait until you win this, so we can get some new decorations and a tree for the center. It will make a world of difference."

Abe still had his wide smile on his face, and he kept it there until her grandmother's friends had left. Once he was sure they weren't overheard, he gave her a thoughtful look. "There's a lot of pressure on you, Lara."

She swallowed. "There's a lot of pressure on Ben, too. We both want this. Likely for the same reasons."

Both of them looked over at the same time to where Ben had his arm around Rudy's neck. It was clear he was giving the kid some kind of pep talk, trying to keep his spirits up, and Lara couldn't ignore the guilt lapping around her.

Ben had been generous. He could have enjoyed the pub- licity of working alongside a former teammate. Truth was, it probably wouldn't have mattered what their snowman looked like. On her own, she couldn't possibly have compet- ed.

A weird kind of siren sounded, grabbing everyone's at- tention. Marty was center stage again. "Time's up. Let's gather our competitors together again and announce to- night's winner."

Lara's smile felt forced, her stomach churning. Marty did his usual, building the anticipation before finally pulling out a gold-colored envelope. Lara could see the tiny bit of hope still in Rudy's eyes, hoping that they might win.

But she already knew. Abe had been magic, and she hoped her own contribution of the upside-down snowmen might have given them the edge. So when Marty yelled and announced them as winners, it didn't come as a surprise.

Had tonight's challenge even been fair or would whoever worked alongside Abe had won regardless?

She couldn't wash away the feeling that Ben had been the bigger player here. Thankfully, Abe continued to keep his sports head in place, and made a fuss over Rudy, offering him a tour of the Vermont Bulls stadium and prime seats at the next game.

Her workmates crowded around her. "You've won two out of the five challenges! Go, girl. You're doing great."

Lara wanted to feel a buzz. She'd expected to feel one. But for some reason, she felt strangely flat. She could see the disappointment on both Rudy and Ben's faces, even though they were both doing their best to hide it.

As her workmates swept her away to go for a few drinks, she cast a glance over her shoulder, lifting her hand and giving Ben a small wave of her hand.

His response was barely noticeable, just a tiny nod of his head. And she pressed her lips together, trying to ignore the strange feeling in the pit of her stomach.

Chapter Ten

"WHAT ON EARTH do you think they're up to now? Do you think it's another quiz?"

Ben and Lara sat opposite each other in a small room cut off from everyone else. They'd been told they would be under a time limit for tonight's challenge, with no outside help.

Lara shrugged. "I have no idea." She pushed the plate of cookies toward him.

He smiled as he lifted one and looked at it. "Is this a distraction technique?"

"It could be. When they told me we'd be locked in a room for more than hour, I decided we needed supplies."

The aroma from the cookie was already enticing. He tried to place it. "Cinnamon, cranberries, and a hint of orange?"

She laughed. "What are you, the Christmas cookie connoisseur?"

He groaned. "Please don't let this be a cookie-making contest. I've already lost two challenges. Tonight is crunch time."

Lara's eyes sparked with recognition. "Of course it is. I hadn't thought about that." She paused for a minute then looked him in the eye. "Well, no matter what the challenge is, good luck."

She was being genuine. He could tell immediately. He'd expected her to come in tonight with more bravado and confidence. But she hadn't at all. She'd been strangely quiet.

"Lara, are you okay?"

She blinked, then licked her lips. "I don't know."

He flinched at her response. "What's wrong?"

"I feel like I had an unfair advantage."

He stilled, putting the cookie back down on the plate. He'd felt that, too. In fact, he'd known it. But he didn't think she'd been so upfront to admit it.

"Why?"

"Because of you, because of Abe. What you did was very generous." She looked down at her interlaced fingers. "I'm not sure if I would have done the same." She pressed her lips together for a few seconds then looked back up. "It was big of you."

He shifted uncomfortably in his chair. "I wasn't trying to be big. I was trying to be fair. Abe offered his services, but I told you, I had Rudy, I wasn't going to turn him away."

She ran one of her hands through her dark hair. "It's just that…"

"What?" Her voice had trailed off as if she didn't want to finish the sentence.

"It's just that, I think—no matter what we'd built— people would have voted for Abe." She gave a little sigh. "I just wish they'd voted for the upside-down snowman." She met his gaze with her brown eyes. "If I win, Ben, I want to win fair and square. Not because my competitor gave me a helping hand."

He understood what she was saying. "I don't love the fact you're beating me. Believe me, tonight, I'm playing to win. My kids need that new gym floor."

She gave a slow, steady nod, her eyes brightening, then held out her hand to him. "Play to win?"

He grinned and shook her hand, letting himself ignore the warmth of her palm in his. "Absolutely."

Marty came in with a pile of pens, pencils, notebooks, and pads. He wasn't holding a microphone tonight, instead he had on a headset and was talking constantly. "So, it's a complete surprise to our contestants that they will have one hour to write us a Christmas story. I've just given them some equipment." He pointed to a camera positioned in the corner of the room to bring it to their attention. "If you want to watch online, you can," he said to the listeners.

They straightened in their seats. Neither had noticed it was there. Lara started wondering if they'd listened in to their earlier conversation.

"So folks, the rules are—there are no rules. It can be a children's story, an adult story, some kind of old legend, or even a spooky story—as long as Christmas is the theme. You have one hour to get something down on paper that we can read to the listeners online, then post on the website. Good luck, folks!"

Marty turned and swept out the door, leaving them both in stunned silence.

"Wow," Ben said, leaning back in his chair. "Not exactly what I expected."

"Me either," Lara said, confusion sweeping over her. Her eyes went to the clock on the wall. "An hour isn't exactly long."

Ben let out a laugh. "Now I know why they confiscated our phones. They don't want us searching for a story."

"I love Christmas, but my mind is entirely blank. I love the thought of some kind of spooky Christmas story, but that kind of thing takes a plan."

"Keep it simple," Ben said as he picked up a pencil. He pulled one of the larger pads toward him, then closed his eyes for a moment.

After a few minutes, Lara put her head on the desk and groaned. "Simple? My brain is doing its best impression of a spider's web. A million different ideas, but nothing rational."

"Who says it needs to be rational?" His eyes glinted as his pencil started to move over the page.

IT WAS ODD. They worked in silence for a while. Ben seemed

really relaxed, settling down into the chair with his hand flying over the page. She tried not to stare, but as soon as she realized he was sketching as well as writing, she was fascinated.

The already-poor plans for some spooky Christmas story just vanished from her head.

"You can draw?" she asked.

He looked up, surprised to find her watching. "I try." He shrugged. "I often have to draw designs for furniture. I hand carve designs, too—you know, bunnies and ducklings into wooden cribs or fishing reels into rocking chairs—just whatever people request. So, I find myself sketching a lot. It's relaxing." He arched an eyebrow. "Some might even call it fun."

His eyes fixed on her page, which had several start lines all scribbled out.

"You need a hand?" Color flooded her cheeks. He'd already helped her once. Last thing she wanted was for him to help her again.

"I'm good," she said quickly, putting her head down and forcing herself to concentrate.

She used to be good at writing essays in school. It had just been a long, long time since she'd done anything like this.

She tried to clear her mind and think about all the things she loved about Christmas. The decorations, the food, the festivities—the aroma of her Christmas cookies. The music and the movies. The wrapping of gifts. The excitement on the faces of kids. The contentment on the faces of those in the home with her grandmother, along with the usual sparkles in their eyes. The kindness of others. That feeling of coming together.

Examples flooded into her head. The way the kids at Ben's high school were all fighting to take part in the competition. Their enthusiasm to win.

The way he'd more or less let her win the other night.

She stopped, her hand freezing above the page. She'd always loved Christmas, but it was odd how her thoughts of Christmas were all now full of Ben. That had never happened before.

Her hand trembled slightly, and she balanced the nib on the page. How did she capture the spirit of Christmas in a story? She looked at her watch—with only thirty minutes left?

Ben's hands flew over his pages, and he had a calm, but dreamy kind of smile. He was loving this. The thought struck like something squeezed at her heart.

If he could do it, she could do it, too.

She bit her lip and started writing, trying to pull every Christmas thought she'd ever had and fit them on the page. When the siren sounded thirty minutes later, she jumped so much she almost fell off her chair.

Marty burst through the door. "And...we're done!"

He bustled over, then lifted the papers from the table.

"Can't wait to read these and see what we've got."

Ben looked every bit as relaxed as before, and that annoyed her, because her heart was thudding furiously against her chest. She'd rushed the last part of her story because she knew she was short on time. Now, she had that horrible sickly feeling. What if it were terrible? The whole world—or at least a good part of Vermont—was about to hear her attempt at a story. How on earth could Ben appear so laid back about this? She tried to catch a glimpse of the pictures in Marty's hand, but he was holding the pages at an odd angle. She'd have to stand up completely to see them, and that would be entirely too obvious.

Was that a pumpkin? In a Christmas story? Her hands grabbed the edges of her chair to keep her bum entirely in place. The temptation to stand up for a better look was strong.

Marty murmured into his headset. "We'll be back after this Christmas music with our stories." He stared at the pages, and Lara knew it wasn't her story he was mesmerized with.

She stood up quickly, "Do we get to come out now?"

One of the other radio staff gave a nod from the door. "Sure, come on through to the studio set. Have a coffee. I imagine it might be fun to listen to your story being read out to the world."

Or not, Lara was tempted to say, but she followed the staffer through to the other side of the studio. Marty and one of the producers scanned the stories, taking pictures to put on the website.

Ben had collected another Christmas cookie and poured them both a coffee, handing her a cup and sitting down on a large sofa.

"You're not nervous?" she asked as she perched next to him, legs jittering.

"Not really," he said, "People either like it, or they don't."

She gave him a sideways look. "You're a bit of dark horse, aren't you? With the drawing—I didn't expect that from you. A man of hidden talents."

He gave a half-laugh. "What—a guy who played baseball and has a woodshop can't draw?"

She couldn't believe how laid back he was about it all. If he lost tonight, then he'd actually lost the whole competition. Shouldn't he be just as nervous as she was?

"Anyway," he said casually. "Drawing might backfire on me. I just had to go with my heart. But people on the radio can't see pictures. Not everyone will go online. This might all work against me."

Her heart gave a leap she would never admit to. She hadn't thought about that. Not for a second. Maybe this wouldn't be such a disaster after all.

Her legs still itched to go look at the pages Ben had sketched. But she did her best job of settling back onto the sofa and trying to look as relaxed as he did while she sipped her coffee.

He was dressed casually in jeans and a red plaid shirt. It suited him. Not that she'd noticed. Not really. She'd never been a girl that liked plaid much, but now…

She tried to snap out of it as the music finished and Marty began talking. He started playing a kind of quiet children's theme in the background as he described Ben's story and started reading. The staffer who filmed the live stream was practically sitting on his shoulder, letting the viewers online see the pictures.

And as much as she hated to admit it—Lara was mesmerized. It was a simple story about a leftover pumpkin who hadn't been used at Halloween and was feeling down because it was now Christmas and his season was over. He watched the family decorate the tree and then wrap the presents while he felt miserable out in the snow. But then, the family realized they didn't have a special box to put their most important present in, and the little boy found the pumpkin. They hollowed him out, then carved Santa and his sleigh into the front, putting the gift inside. On Christmas morning, the rest of the family found the picture of their new little brother or sister who would be joining them for Christmas next year, then put candles inside the pumpkin who had center stage on the table for Christmas dinner. It was clever. It had an underlying message for kids that said even if it wasn't their season, there was always a place at the table for them. By the time it finished, Lara had tears in her eyes and her hand over her mouth. "It's wonderful," she said, turning to Ben.

He gave a smile. "Turns out I have two favorite times of year. I just wanted to combine them."

She looked at him, and saw a whole lot more behind those green eyes than he was saying out loud. It was even some of the terminology in the story. A season. The message. About not being their season and always having a place at the table. It was him. His baseball career coming to an abrupt end with his injury, he had to find a new place, a new career.

She reached over and gave his hand a squeeze. She didn't need him to say anything out loud. She wanted him to know she understood.

The applause in the studio came to an end, and Marty started reading her story. It was pale in comparison to Ben's, clearly rushed in places.

Her story started with a young woman running off the road in a snowdrift on Christmas Eve and stumbling upon a ramshackle house. But as she arrived, she smelled Christmas food cooking. When she pushed open the door, she found a handsome young man waiting for her. A fire was roaring, and she was able to warm up and have some food.

He was charming and introduced himself as Robin. Polite and well-mannered, he treated her well—even if his clothes were a little old fashioned. She was on her way back home to meet her boyfriend—who didn't treat her quite so well. Before she left, Robin gave her a gentle kiss.

When she gets back to her car, she found it had been pulled from the ditch and the road had been cleared, but instead of heading back home, she turned around and headed in the opposite direction. When she saw a plaque at the side of road, she stopped to read it. It commemorated *The house for lost people,* which burned down on Christmas Eve, 1888, killing its owner Robin Barclay. He often took in waifs and strays to help get them on the right path. The story ended as the young women realized exactly who she'd met and blew him a kiss, which floated through the snowflakes landing around her.

Lara's hand was still wrapped around Ben's. She hadn't even noticed until he returned her squeeze. "Spooky, I liked it."

She let out the breath that she'd been holding for the longest time, cringing as her words were read on the airwaves. It wasn't quite as bad as she'd thought. She wasn't going to die of embarrassment.

One of the staffers came over, her face full of excitement as she glanced between them. "The phone lines and internet are going crazy. A children's story and a romance?" She shook her head in admiration. "People are going to say we planned this and had this all done in advance. Honestly, we couldn't have planned things any better. You two are just publicity dynamite." Her eyes fell on their clasped hands, and she smirked and raised her eyebrows without saying another word.

Lara quickly pulled her hand back, sticking it under her other arm as if hiding it away. "I'm just glad I didn't humiliate myself," she said. "I nearly had a mad panic attack in that room when you were practically lying horizontal sketching that story—you were so laid back about it."

"You did?" He seemed surprised.

"Of course I did. Talk about pressure. You were writing like crazy, and I didn't have a single coherent idea in my head."

He waved out his hand. "Seems like you did." He folded his arms across his chest. "And here I thought you were trying to distract me with those Christmas cookies. Anyway, shouldn't it be me who's under pressure? You're in the lead. If I fail tonight, the competition is over."

She shook her head. "No way. You've nailed it. There will probably be a publisher on the phone in less than an hour."

Marty came back over. "Well, you two know how to light up the airwaves. Come through to the studio so we can interview you. It seems like our audience can't get enough of you tonight."

Lara pulled out her phone, then clicked on the radio website. Comments were pouring in. Literally—hundreds of them.

She turned her phone around so Ben could see. "Hope you're feeling the love."

His brow wrinkled and he leaned forward, his fingertips

brushing hers as he took her phone. She watched as his face lit up in a smile before he nudged her. "Look, people love your story just as much as mine," he said, pointing at a complimentary comment.

She laughed and nudged him back. "I think you'll find you have ten times as many comments as I do."

One of the staffers appeared, holding a bottle of champagne and two glasses. "It's on us," she said. "The producers are having a kitten about how successful this has been."

Before either of them had a chance to think, they were both holding a glass of champagne in their hands. "Okay," Lara said. "I'm going to call this. You're the runaway winner today, so hats off to you." She gave a cheeky glance "I didn't know you had it in you, but my grandmother always warned me to never underestimate my opponent. So, here's to a fun time for the rest of the competition."

Ben watched her through those thick dark lashes. Those brown eyes could be hypnotic. And she couldn't pretend she didn't like them.

She pulled over the plate loaded with the rest of the Christmas cookies that she'd made. Someone from the crew must have brought them through from the other room, and they'd done some serious damage to the pile—there were only a few left.

"Guess we might as well finish these," she said.

"Still think you're trying to distract me," Ben said. He paused for a second and then smiled. "And it might be working."

A little shiver stole down her spine as they clinked their glasses together.

This Christmas contest became more interesting every day.

Chapter Eleven

H E WON BY a landslide—and couldn't help the swell of pride he felt in his chest after the roar of celebration from the kids.

The story and sketches had just flown from his fingertips without much thought. It had been instinct.

Now, he waited patiently to hear what the fourth challenge would be.

"This time, guys, we want you to pick your favorite Christmas song—traditional or otherwise—and gather a choir to sing it. Your choir will perform in two nights time, so get to practicing!"

The high school kids cheered. It was obvious they were going to be his choir. Although, his gut told him, that a few wouldn't want to be involved.

Worry lines creased Lara's head. "What's wrong?" he asked.

She took a deep breath. "I'm not sure about this."

"Why not? Can't you use some of people from the hospital? Or your grandmother and her friends?"

Lara shifted uncomfortably. "I'm not sure that's the right

thing to do. It seems kind of…exploitive."

Ben gave a thoughtful nod. "It's up to you. You've got to do what feels right." He nudged. "We have a deal, remember? In it to win it."

When she turned to face him, her eyes were sparkling. Just the way he liked them, and his stomach gave a flip.

Being around Lara was addictive. Her smile. The smell of her perfume. The way she mulled things over. The way she twiddled a strand of hair around her finger while she concentrated. All little things he'd noticed about her.

Abe had dropped him a text the other night—congratulating him on the story and telling him not to let something good slip through his fingers.

They hadn't discussed her. But he knew exactly what Abe meant. The guy could read the atmosphere between Ben and Lara twenty paces away.

But she was his competitor. There had already been a few comments when that unsuspecting photo hit the papers. Lara had been horrified, and Ben didn't want to put her in that position again.

There were only a few more days left in the competition. Maybe, just maybe, there could be an opportunity afterward to get to know each other a little better.

He sighed as his phone beeped.

"Something wrong?" she asked.

"Delayed delivery." He sighed. "It's wood I need for a project. I've been so busy I don't have any supplies left." He shook his head at the text. "Apparently, the delivery company is having problems because of the snowfall."

Lara held up her hand. "But it's Vermont. Snow is our default position."

"Seems like we're the only people who know that." He ran his fingers through his hair. "The choir idea is nice, but…"

"But what?"

He lifted both hands. "Truth is, I barely have time for this. When on earth can I rehearse with the kids? I'm already behind at the workshop. Sleep is turning into an optional extra."

"Need a hand?"

He turned toward her, half in shock. "What?"

She laughed. "Well, obviously, I can't make anything for you. But I can answer your emails. Check your orders. Do some admin work for you."

"You'd do that?"

She shrugged. "Why not? You said you're overwhelmed."

His gaze narrowed. "Lara, starting to think you'd do anything to get out of arranging your choir…"

She gave the slightest pause and he wondered if he'd just hit the nail on the proverbial head. He reached forward and squeezed her hand. "You know, the folks in your grandmother's home might love this. It could lift their spirits. Give them something else to focus on rather than the fact their place doesn't have the decorations it usually does."

She bit her lip. He could almost see her thinking. Finally, she sighed and said, "It probably would."

"Then don't be afraid—just do it."

She held up her hands. "But what on earth will they sing?"

He laughed. "Oh, don't have illusions of grandeur. I already know I'll get no say at all in what the kids sing. Know your place. Let your choir decide."

She laughed, too. "You're right, of course you are." She paused for a second, "Thanks, Ben."

"Thank you too," he said. "It was a kind offer. But we both have jobs to do. Let's just do the best we can."

It was like someone had wrapped a warm blanket around her to let her know they understood. The contest started out as fun—and parts of it were. But it also hovered like a rain cloud over her head, making her wonder if she actually would be able to win, and deliver to the people in her grandmother's home. She hated the thought of getting their hopes up, only for them to be dashed.

And Ben was in exactly the same position with his kids in the high school. He probably was the only other person on the planet who understood how she felt right now. And for that, she was grateful.

She started to walk to the door, her coat in her hand, but as she reached it, she turned around and gave him a thoughtful look. "Good luck," she said quietly. And she meant it.

Chapter Twelve

BEN WAS ASTONISHED. It was like he'd hardly needed to talk out loud. The kids had embraced the thought of being part of a choir in a way he hadn't even imagined.

He'd been right. Some of the quieter kids hadn't wanted to be involved. The thought of singing or performing on the radio or live stream had them running for the doors. But not running completely. Most were happy to take part in the background by putting together the music recording or helping choreograph a dance routine.

The kids who did want to take part loudly debated what song they wanted to sing. Ben quickly realized his opinion wasn't really required.

"*Away In A Manger?*" he tried.

He was met with scowls and rolling eyes.

"Something more modern then? Up tempo?"

He listed some songs from the charts over the last few years. But there didn't seem to be one that captured all of their attention. After an hour of arguing, he decided it was time to intervene.

"Why don't we try something new? Something original?"

"Or something old but updated," Mari said quietly.

A dozen heads spun toward her and she visibly shied back, surprised by the reaction to her comment. Ben smiled. "I think Mari might be right."

Rudy wrinkled his nose, but Ben kept going. "Think about it. You could start the song in the traditional way with singing, then mix it up a little in the middle, add in some rap, before finishing it in the traditional way again—or not, depending what you decide."

The kids all started looking at each other, trying to decide if this was a good idea—or a bad one.

"Which song will we start with?" Luke asked. He had a portable keyboard in his lap.

After a few seconds, the rest crowded around him. Ben sat back, his smile spreading. He was so lucky. This was a great bunch of kids. They might not be playing sports right now—and singing would never be his specialty—but the enthusiasm and inclusion-for-everyone aspect were the things he'd worked hardest on with these kids. And they were demonstrating it in spades.

He couldn't be prouder. So, he stayed exactly where he was and let them take the lead. Like a mentor should.

LARA WAS BEING bombarded on every side. She actually didn't know which way to look.

"I'm in charge," Mrs. Armstrong shouted. "I led the church choir for years!"

"That screechy old bunch?" Harry Fielding said. "There's no way we're sounding like that."

"I can play the piano," Eve Robinson said quietly.

"We need a guitar!" Reg Dean shouted. "In fact, let's make it mainly instrumental. Then we might have a half a chance of winning. We can all just hum along."

One of the nurses folded her arms next to Lara. "Bet you never realized just how unruly this lot could be."

"Not for a second," Lara breathed as she watched her grandmother get into another argument with the woman across the room.

"I get to decide what we sing," she said loudly. "It's my granddaughter who's in charge. She's the one who got us into this contest."

"Hmph," the other woman grunted. "If she'd won the first three challenges, we wouldn't need to do this one."

Lara sighed and put her head on the nurse's shoulder. "What on earth do I do?"

The nurse laughed. "You have no idea how glad I am that this is not my problem. For me, this is an everyday reaction. I'm just so glad it's you who has to deal with them, and not me." She raised her eyebrows. "My advice? Get into the middle of it, and take charge. They generally just like shouting at each other. Not at us—or you. And feel free to tell them to behave." She nudged Lara. "Some of them think they can use their age as an excuse for bad behavior."

"My grandmother among them?"

The nurse tapped the side of her nose. "I'm saying nothing. But go on. Be the boss."

Lara's stomach squeezed. This had seemed like a good idea at first. Instead, it felt like trying to herd cats. How on earth could she manage this?

"Go on, Lara," she muttered to herself. "This might be fun. You could enjoy it," she said with her jaw more than a little clenched as she repeated Ben's words. "Where are you when I might actually need you, Ben Winters?" she asked as she took the fateful steps to the center of the room.

She clapped her hands loudly. "Enough! We don't have time for this fighting. We need to pick a song and start practicing, and we need to do it now." She put her hands on her hips and spun around, catching the gaze of all the faces and trying to appear much braver than she felt. "If you want to take part, then thank you very much. If you don't want to take part—then that's fine. But I don't want anyone who'll disrupt our practice time. Is that clear?"

She sounded like a schoolteacher. And she kind of liked it. She tilted her chin upward, daring any to challenge her, but secretly hoping they wouldn't.

The nurse had given her an old CD player, with a CD that had numerous Christmas tunes on it, so she pressed play and started the first song. "Okay, everyone, let's sing along and get a feel for things. We'll try a few to see how everyone feels about it. We can take a vote later to pick the best one."

Initially, there was an uncomfortable silence. Then, Beatrice, the nurse, started singing loudly at the top of her voice, giving Lara a wink. She didn't have the greatest voice, but at least it encouraged the rest to join in.

Lara gave her a grateful nod. They had to start somewhere.

Two hours later, her throat was sore and she was exhausted. They'd already stopped for tea, and more arguments had ensued over people deliberately trying to sabotage songs.

"You knew that was my favorite. You deliberately sung off key!"

"You wouldn't know what off key was. You're flat for every song."

"If you call that harmonizing, you live in cloud cuckoo land."

"We should be trying something better. This is all boring."

Lara sighed and tried to paste a smile on her face. At this rate, they would still be fighting over the song choice tomorrow.

What was decidedly clear was that her choir needed to practice. Some were good and some were just enthusiastic. She wasn't quite sure how to get the best out of them.

She turned back to the bare courtyard and swallowed. This time of year, it should be decorated with the huge tree and twinkling lights. The place seemed bare without it.

Usually, most of the activities at this time of year would take place around the gorgeous central courtyard. Now, it was like everyone was purposely ignoring the fact there was nothing to enjoy. But it also felt like a bit of Christmas spirit had been lost from the place. Lara knew that the staff was doing their best, but even their smiles weren't quite so bright this year.

It made her heart feel heavy. She *had* to get this right. She had to win this challenge. If she closed her eyes, she could remember their excited faces last year. She wanted that again. They deserved it. And she would do her absolute best to fight to get it for them.

Ben would understand. He would. And, hopefully, they could still be friends. Maybe she could help him try and fundraise some other way for the school gym?

She took a breath and another sip of tea, straightening her shoulders and going back into the room. It felt kind of like being Daniel in the lion's den. But decisions had to be made.

"Okay, everyone, let's take a vote. We've tried ten different songs. It's time to pick the one we can perform best tomorrow night. Now, remember, don't just pick your favorite—pick the one that sounded best."

She was met with a few murmurs of dissent. But she could take that. After a few colorful minutes, the vote was called. Lara sighed in relief. She wasn't even sure how good they could make it, but at least they'd made a decision.

She gave them all an enthusiastic round of applause as Beatrice came over. "Right, folks, you've voted fairly on a song. Everyone remember that Lara has to work tomorrow. But I'm here for the day shift, so we can all practice while she's at work, then have a final rehearsal before the radio show tomorrow night."

She put her hands on Lara's shoulders and laughed. "Breathe, Lara. You've gotten through the worst of it. I'll help you from here."

"Thank you," Lara breathed out in relief.

"It's done them good," Beatrice said as she scanned the room. "Even the fighting. It's given them something to argue and be passionate about, and even though you probably don't know it, it has lifted their mood. So thank you."

"No," Lara said quickly. "Thank you for doing so much for my grandmother and her friends."

Beatrice gave her a mischievous look. "So, while we're chatting, want to tell me what's going on between you and our resident hunk?"

Lara's mouth fell open. "Nothing. Nothing's happening."

"Oh, pull the other one. Are you crazy? Half of Vermont knows he exists now. If you don't get in there quick, someone else will beat you to it."

Lara bit the inside of her cheek. She wasn't crazy about the thought of half of Vermont coming to look for Ben Winters.

"We're just friends. Or enemies. Or something." She waved her hand, getting flustered.

Beatrice laughed again, her eyes understanding. "He's lovely, Lara, and so are you. From where I'm standing, you look like a perfect match. Don't let this competition get between you. This is temporary. Ben Winters? Now, he could be permanent."

Heat rushed through Lara as Beatrice walked away. She leaned back against the wall for a moment, taking a few breaths. He made her laugh. He made her smile. On the few occasions he'd touched her skin, it had sent wild crazy shots of electricity through her.

He was thoughtful, and she'd already seen a side of his nature that made her sure he was a good human being. But what did he think of her?

She pressed her lips together. It was only a few more days until the contest ended. Hopefully, she'd find out then.

Chapter Thirteen

B EN WAS FRANTIC. The phone hadn't stopped. He'd had to make a dozen calls to try to find a new supplier who could deliver in time for Christmas. His muscles ached. He'd started at five this morning, and he intended to come back after rehearsals and the performance at the contest. There just weren't enough hours in the day right now. The work was getting to be too much for just one person, and all he had in the woodshop for company was the radio.

As the phone rang once again, right in the middle of a crucial fixture on a rocking chair, he almost let out a curse. But it stopped midway in his throat when he heard a female voice say, "Winters Woodshop, how can I help you?"

He froze. He recognized that voice. Lara?

He bent forward as she rounded the corner, the phone still in her hand. "If you give me a moment, I'll check that right out for you."

She smiled as her coat brushed against some old wood shavings and came away covered. "Ben..." One eyebrow arched as if to say I-told-you-so. "Will the McQuillop's order be ready for pick up tomorrow?"

He cast his eyes over his shoulder to the handmade wooden cabinet that had its second set of varnish drying. "Yep, it will be ready."

She answered smartly, then put down the phone and surveyed the chaos around her—the first part being Ben.

She walked over and put her hand on her hips. "Did you eat this morning?"

He shook his head. "No time." But then he tilted his head. "Lara, what are you doing here?"

She lifted on hand. "We'll get to that—but it's not important. It can wait. Let me deal with a few issues first."

She disappeared, then came back ten minutes later with coffee, sandwiches, and muffins from their favorite coffee store. Ben couldn't help but smile in relief as the aroma of coffee and freshly baked goods swept toward him.

She sat them down on a central bench, and pulled out a black notebook. "Okay, for the next hour, we both work and eat. I'll go through your work emails, take notes, and answer any calls. At the end of that, I'll hit you with a list of questions that you can answer while you work."

The words were like music to his soul. The last few days, he'd felt as if he were slowly drowning in the woodshop. This was his place. His pleasure. His sanctuary. And those feelings had slowly but surely been ebbing away.

"Lara—" he started, but she held up her hand and stopped him. "They gave me the day off from work to get ready for tonight, but when I got to the care center, I realized

SCARLET WILSON

the nurse, Beatrice, had things well in hand and I shouldn't
interfere. I came here to get you to mend something…" She
gave a soft smile. "But it turns out it's you who needs
mending, so anything else can wait." She held out both
hands. "Let me do what I can. Don't talk—just work and
eat." She rolled her eyes. "Believe me, in an hour's time,
you'll be praying for me to shut up."

"I don't believe that for a second," Ben said as he broke
all the rules and grabbed his muffin first. "But thank you for
being here. I appreciate it."

The edges of her lips turned upward. Lara smiled a lot,
but this time, her smile was only for him.

She gave him a nod of her head and picked up her coffee,
settling at the desk and lifting open the laptop.

"Password?" she yelled above the noise that had already
started.

Ben shoved some hair out of his eyes and cringed.
"Woodshop," he shouted back.

She didn't say a word—just let her eyebrows send the
message.

He carried on working. Even though the hum of the
tools and the background noise of the radio were there, he
was conscious of her every move. Whenever she answered the
phone and spoke to someone, whenever she moved around
the woodshop with a chart in her hand as if she were taking
an inventory, the smell of her orange-scented perfume
floated gently through the air, fighting for space among the

170

traditional woody aromas.

Every time he breathed in, he could smell her. It was intoxicating.

Almost exactly on the hour, she appeared with her shiny black notebook in hand. She'd pulled her hair up into a ponytail and was wearing a black skirt and a bright pink shirt—obviously her work clothes.

He took a second to glance down at his t-shirt and work trousers, which were covered in varying degrees of sawdust and wood chips.

She didn't let him speak. "Okay, we'll go through this in various ways. First, we'll do the orders you've agreed to, and that are still outstanding. Then, we'll do stock and supplies." She gave him a sheet. "I've made you an inventory list."

He didn't even get a chance to finish before she started again. "Then we'll do emails and messages, and I'll follow them up. Then, we'll chat through potential new orders and you can decide if you have capacity to do them. Then…" She paused and bit her lip, fixing her brown eyes on him. "Then we'll talk about the funding for a new scheme in Vermont about apprenticeships. You need help around here, Ben. And this could be a perfect training opportunity for someone."

He swallowed and looked around the woodshop. Of course. He'd never really given it any thought. There hadn't been time to.

"Sit down," she said. She'd pulled one of his handmade

chairs over next to the office desk. "We can do this in half an hour."

He smiled as he moved over beside her, letting himself inhale as he stood close enough to see the tiny freckles scattered over her nose. "Has anyone ever told you that you can be a bit bossy?"

She blinked, not moving but obviously enjoying the fact they were closer than normal. "I'm not bossy, I'm organized, and Ben... You need organized right now."

He wasn't going to argue about that. There was no point because it was entirely true. She smiled and put her hand up, resting it on his arm. Her palm against his skin felt like a beacon of warmth on a snowy day. "I'm good at this. Let me help you. I have a little bit of time today."

She made perfect sense. He knew she did. He wasn't the kind of guy who would ever ask anyone for help. When he hadn't made it in baseball, he hadn't wanted any handouts or favors. He'd been determined to find his own new career path—and he had... through hard work.

But Ben wasn't a dummy. Something had to change around here, or he would miss orders and lose his good reputation. He wasn't fool enough to look the proverbial gift horse in the mouth. And his gift horse was the gorgeous Lara Cottridge.

Her hand was still on his arm. "Thank you, Lara. I appreciate this."

She tilted her head up toward him. He was tempted. Oh

boy, he was tempted to lean forward and capture her lips with his. And just as he had that thought, she licked her pink lips. He held his breath, wondering if she were having the same thought.

Right now, he didn't want this moment to end.

She was looking at him with those brown eyes. The ones he felt as if he could stare into forever. He was clearly crazy. Absolutely losing his mind. Because this wasn't him. This had never been him.

But then, he'd never met Lara before. A girl who had as much passion and loyalty as him.

Her fingers flinched a little, tightening on his skin, before she swallowed and took a step back, color flushing her cheeks. "Let's get started," she said as she tugged at her skirt and sat back down on the chair.

"Let's get started," he repeated slowly.

He'd never heard finer words.

Chapter Fourteen

"WHAT'S WRONG?" HER grandmother asked the question for the third time, and Lara shifted uncomfortably.

"Nothing," she said quickly as she slid a woolen blanket onto her grandmother's lap.

Beatrice had arranged the transport of the residents with military precision. No one would get to leave here without being properly attired for the weather outside. It was only a short ten-minute walk to the hall where the choir contest was being held. But the temperature had fallen again, and thick snowflakes were already floating down from the dark sky.

Her grandmother's frail hand reached out and grabbed her wrist. "Ouch." Her grandmother's skin was almost transparent, the blue veins clearly visible underneath. But her grip was still surprisingly strong.

"Don't tell me *nothing*. I'm not stupid, Lara."

Lara pressed her lips together, then sat down next to her grandmother's chair. She wasn't quite sure what to say, because she hadn't made sense of everything in her own mind yet.

"I spent most of today with Ben," she said.

"You did?" Her grandmother looked surprised. "You weren't working?"

She shook her head. "They let me off work. I came in here, but Beatrice said the rehearsals were going well. So I picked up the newspaper holder—you know, the wooden one that's been broken for a while—and took it to Ben's woodshop to see if he could fix it."

Her grandmother released her wrist, then folded her hands in her lap. "I don't see it anywhere," she said.

Lara groaned and shook her head. "I never even got a chance to ask him to fix it. When I got there—things were in chaos. His phone kept ringing, he had one hundred and forty unopened emails on his work laptop, and about forty enquiries on his website." She threw her hands up. "He was there by himself. Every piece he makes is handcrafted. He just wasn't getting a chance to do the job he should, so I offered to help him."

"And?"

Lara sighed. "And... I'm not sure I should spend another day around Ben Winters."

Her grandmother was as sharp as a tack. "Why? In case he captures you with his winter spell?"

Lara couldn't help but laugh. "It might be too late," she admitted.

"Lara?" The voice was full of compassion. Lara looked up into her grandmother's face. "If you find something worth holding on to..." Her grandmother reached over and squeezed Lara's hands. "Then hold on to it. If that's the only thing I ever teach you, then that's enough."

Lara half stood and hugged her grandmother. "Oh, you've taught me every single thing that's important. Don't doubt it for a minute."

Her grandmother's eyes gleamed. "Then what are we waiting for? Take me to the place so I can see your potential young man."

❧

THE KIDS WERE bouncing off the walls. They'd been practicing all afternoon, and Ben hadn't got tired of watching or listening to them. He had the easy part—all he had to do was start the music and cross his fingers that everything went to plan.

Their enthusiasm was infectious. The whole room was buzzing, and he was just glad he could be part of it.

After a final rehearsal, the kids all bundled up in their outerwear and headed for the town hall. Only eight of the kids were actually performing, but that didn't mean the rest didn't want to come watch. A few of the other staff from the school were coming, too, all to support the kids.

Rudy led the way as they skipped along the street toward the hall. Ben could see the competition coming from the other direction. Several of the people from the care home were being pushed in chairs, Lara's red coat easy to pick out amongst the crowd. She was leaning forward to talk in the ear of the person she was pushing—it must be her grand-mother.

"Be mannerly," Ben reminded the kids. But he needn't have bothered. The kids mingled among their rivals easily, chattering away. He could see that some of the older com-petitors were equally happy to chat with the young people. There was laughter and teasing, along with a few more intense-looking conversations.

Caleb wandered over next to him and pointed at a man in a wheelchair. "Mr. Armstrong was an aeronautical engi-neer. He's got some great stories."

Ben patted him on the shoulder. "Maybe we can arrange for you two to chat again sometime."

"Really?"

"Sure. Let me find out if that's something we can sort out."

He wandered among the rest of the people. There was a much bigger crowd tonight. It was clear the competition was picking up more and more interest.

It only took a few moments to find himself next to Lara. "Okay?" he asked.

She nodded, brushing her hair behind her ear. "Good, thanks." She glanced at the bright-eyed woman in the chair she was pushing, but before she got a chance to say anything, the white-haired lady thrust her hand toward Ben.

"Edith Cottridge. You must be Ben Winters." She gave Lara a knowing glance. "I've heard a lot about you."

He shook her hand firmly, knowing the quip was designed to disarm him. "Pleasure to meet you, ma'am. I've heard a lot about you, too."

Edith smiled, knowing immediately he was on to her.

She patted the seat next to her. "Well, sit down here, young man. We've clearly got a lot of catching up to do."

Lara stepped between them. "I don't think we have time. We have to get you all set up for the choir, and Ben has to organize his kids, too."

There was a half-pleading tone in her voice, and he could tell she was panicking. He wasn't quite sure who she was trying to save here. Ben, her grandmother, or herself?

It didn't really matter. He gave a nod to Edith. "Why don't we try and catch up later?"

Edith didn't miss a trick and wagged her finger at him with a gleam in her eye. "That's if I'm still talking to you, of course. I'm here to win."

He laughed out loud. "Now I know where you get it from," he said to Lara.

She smiled back at him as she steered Edith away, "You're right, of course, all the best bits come from my grandmother."

THE HALL WAS getting busier and busier. It was decided the assisted living residents would go first because it took longer to get them set up. Under their coats, they were all wearing Christmas sweaters, and Harry Fielding had even managed to wrap some lights around his chair. Beatrice had a whole array of Santa hats, which she passed out.

When they were all ready, Lara stood at the front and nervously licked her lips. Ben was leaning against a pillar with his arms folded, watching her with a casual expression on his face. He didn't seem to get flustered about anything. It was darn annoying.

Marty did the introductions, then handed over the reins. There was no ancient tape recorder. The studio had managed to get hold of a piano and Mrs. Armstrong perched on the stool, hands poised, ready to play.

Lara waved her hands and counted out loud, "One, two, three."

The tinkling noise started. There were no wrong notes. Mrs. Armstrong played perfectly, and *Silent Night* reverberated around the room. Lara couldn't help but smile as the voices started, at first a little shaky, then building confidence and volume as the song progressed. They actually harmonized together. It was beautiful. Their voices were full of the lives they had lived—their experiences, their joys, and their heartaches—and it was all there, for everyone to hear.

Lara couldn't help the tears that formed in her eyes—happy tears—as they moved toward the finish. She was so proud of her grandmother and her friends for taking part. When the last note fell away, the crowd erupted into applause.

She could see the students shooting slightly panicked glances at Ben. But he just shook his head, and gestured with his hand for them to stay calm.

Marty was talking wildly, and Lara took the time to go around to everyone in her choir to give them a hug. "You were fabulous," she whispered in each of their ears.

She wasn't even listening to what Marty was saying because once they were finished, she had to help clear the floor again, positioning the wheelchairs where their occupants would be able to see the students perform.

It took a bit of time, but when Marty started talking again, giving the introduction for the kids from Briarhill Falls High, Ben waved to the kids to take their positions on the floor.

The lights dimmed, and Lara almost laughed as she sucked in a breath.

Then, the music started, this time via a phone and speaker.

Her skin gave a tingle as she recognized the tune immediately. It was *Silent Night*, too—the kids had picked the same song. That was why Ben had been signaling to them.

But their version of *Silent Night* was entirely different. It started traditionally, with one clear voice. After a few lines, the other voices were added in one by one. It was effective.

Then, as they finished the first verse, the tempo changed and the lights came on. One of the kids—Rudy—had a microphone and started rapping as the kids behind him danced. It was modern. It was bright. People in the audience started clapping along. The up-tempo version was definitely attracting attention. Lara could see just how hard the kids had practiced. Ben watched their every move. Was his body even moving a little—mirroring the routine? She grinned.

The kids spun, striking a pose, and the lights dimmed again. And there it was again. That one voice, singing the final few lines in the traditional way.

Perfect. A blend of both past and present.

When the song finished, Lara couldn't help but clap and cheer along with everyone else. Ben walked into the middle of the floor, arms wide, wrapping all the kids in a bear hug. Their joy was infectious.

Marty appeared at the side, telling the listeners how they could vote and that they only had thirty minutes to get them in. But Lara knew in her heart what was about to happen.

She wrapped her hands around her grandmother's neck and whispered in her ear. "You were brilliant. You were all brilliant."

Her grandmother reached up and squeezed Lara's hand. "Thank you for this, honey. It's meant so much to us."

Lara brushed a tear away. "But we might not win."

"We've already won—even if we don't get the money. You've given us our Christmas spirit back."

Marty was clearly excited. One of the staffers moved over next to Lara.

"Heard the news?" she said in a low voice.

Lara shook her head.

"Marty thinks he's in line for one the big jobs at a national station. This competition has made him extremely popular."

"Really?" She didn't mean to sound quite so surprised. "Great. He's done a really good job."

The staffer gave a wry laugh. "No. You and Ben have done a really good job. If we'd gotten different contestants, this competition probably would have faded pretty quickly."

"You think?"

The staffer gave her a strange look. "I know. You two are dynamite."

And just like that, Lara's mouth went instantly dry. Her first reaction was to try to deny everything. But she didn't get a chance. The staffer just gave her an appreciative nod before walking off.

By the time the announcement was ready to be made, the atmosphere in the room was electric. Nothing had dampened in the half hour in between. Ben stood among his students, but she couldn't pretend not to notice his eyes were definitely on her.

Lara's grandmother gave her a knowing smile. "Nice boy."

There was no point trying to deny how she felt. "I think

so," she admitted.

It was odd. But even though the competition had introduced her to Ben, in a way, she couldn't wait for it to be over. At least then, she could see how they really were around each other—how much they had in common and if this attraction were mutual.

Because she really, *really* hoped it was.

Marty appeared again with his well-used golden envelope. Part of Lara's stomach still held a little bit of hope. Both of the performances had been good. But when Marty looked over at Ben's group and shouted out, "Briarhill Falls High is the winner," she couldn't really be sad.

As the crowd continued to mingle, Ben came over to her side. For the first time, he leaned forward and kissed her cheek. "You put up an admirable fight. Your grandmother's choir was excellent."

"Thank you," she said, a little stunned by his action.

"No," he said. "Thank you for today. If you hadn't helped me, I probably would have drowned back there. You didn't need to, and I appreciate it."

Heat warmed through her. "What are friends for?" she said simply.

Something flashed in his eyes, and the smile that spread across his face seemed to be just for her.

"Friends," he said. "I like that."

"So do I."

He gave a small nod. "But will you remember it tomorrow, when it's all down to the final challenge?"

"Of course," she breathed.

He winked at her. "I'll hold you to it."

Chapter Fifteen

"I NEVER THOUGHT for a minute I'd be back here," Ben said.

Lara laughed as she stood alongside him. "Santa's Grotto," she said, her breath clouding the air around them.

Santa's Grotto was busy. It was always busy. It appeared every year in the town square, with a large entrance to where the kids got to meet Santa's elves and another room where they could meet Santa.

"I remember this from when I was a kid," Lara said, "When I visited my grandmother." She couldn't wipe the smile from her face. "I loved it. I thought it was real."

Ben stood with his hands in his jean pockets. After a few moments, he gave a reluctant nod. "So did I," he admitted.

She laughed. "Okay, then. Let's check out the tree."

There was always a tree in the middle of Santa's Grotto. Over the years, it had collected a whole range of different Christmas ornaments. Lara held her hand up next to a beautiful clear glass bauble with a blue glass snowflake inside it. "Some of these are stunning," she breathed.

Ben nodded as he slowly walked around the tree, taking

in the wide range of ornaments – some from all over the world.

They both inched their way around the tree, meeting back at the same point. Lara pulled a face. "How on earth are we supposed to make our own—entirely original—ornament for the tree? They've already got everything."

Ben took his time before answering. "I guess there's always something new."

She knew her face was still crumpled. "This is going to be tough."

He looked down at her. "Ten thousand dollars tough?"

It was like a little chill blowing over her skin. Of course.

"I guess I'll need to wrack my brain then," she said slowly.

"We both will." There was something in the way he said it. Ben was always cool, calm, and collected. But somehow, she knew he already had something in his brain that he could use. Her stomach lurched, her heart squeezing.

Lara still wanted to play to win. She didn't want to give up without a fight.

"I'm going to stay a while longer," she said determinedly. "I want to make sure I don't repeat something that's already there."

He gave a brief nod. "I need to head back to the wood-shop." He hesitated before meeting her gaze. "Maybe I'll catch up with you later?" There was a definite hopeful tone in his voice.

"Sure," she said. Part of her wanted to concentrate fully on making the best tree decoration possible to win the contest. But part of her was jumping forward a couple of days, wishing this was all over and waiting to see if anything could happen between her and Ben.

And waiting was excruciating.

He gave her a wave as he trudged out into the snow. She watched him all the way along the street—wishing she could join him.

❧

IT WAS IN his hand. And it was perfect.

All he had to do was hollow out a little hole at either side so it could hang from the tree.

As soon as he'd looked at the tree full of items from across the world, he knew exactly what he would make.

It could be considered cheating because he'd already made it. He'd been working on this set—on and off—for years. This was the final piece.

He held it in the palm of his hand. Hand-carved from wood grown right here in Vermont was the baby Jesus in a cradle. He'd put the finishing touches on it a few nights ago before going to bed.

It was probably old-fashioned, but it contained a piece of Ben's heart. He'd started this set years ago, carving one or two pieces a year, after he'd constructed the manger. Some pieces were better than others. The first shepherd was a little rough. But he'd learned more as he'd created. Last year, it had been Mary and Joseph—Mary sitting on a stool, peering down to look in the cradle, with Joseph beside her with a hand out-stretched on Mary's shoulder. This year, he'd carved the angel Gabriel and baby Jesus in the cradle, finishing them both with some varnish.

He took out his tools and smiled. He'd have to carve another baby Jesus in the cradle to complete the set, but that could happen next year. He slowly and delicately made two tiny holes at either end of the cradle, ready to be threaded.

He didn't have a doubt that this was what he should use. It might not be the most flashy or colorful decoration, but it was pure him. And he was proud of it.

He tucked it back into his pocket, then spent the next few hours finishing up a few other jobs before locking up the workshop and heading back to the Grotto. The decoration didn't need to be hung on the tree until tomorrow morning, but Lara had said she might stay longer. He didn't want her to be there alone. He headed down the street, glancing at his watch along the way.

The lights were still on in the Grotto at the end of the lane, so he stopped to pick up some coffee and cookies for them both.

"Lara?" he said as he pushed the door open.

The lights were dim, giving off a pale orange glow. The main entryway was empty—apart from the tree and decorations—so he carried the steaming coffee cups through to where Santa usually met with the kids.

She was bent over a table, her face screwed up in concentration, a bright white light illuminating whatever she was doing.

It was clear she hadn't heard him call out. He didn't want to alarm her, so he waited a few moments, letting the smell of coffee and cookies drift toward her until she finally lifted her head.

"Hey," he said quietly.

She spun around in the chair. "Hey," she said, a smile stealing across her face. "I didn't even hear you come in."

He gestured toward the table. "You were concentrating." He held up the cups and cookie bag. "I wasn't even sure if you'd still be here. Do you know what time it is?"

She shook her head and glanced at her watch. "Oops. Ali—one of the elves—, she left a little while ago. I told her I'd only be another half hour. She said she'd lock the place up once I was gone."

She leaned back in the chair, and he watched as she took a deep breath. "There's something kind of magical about being in Santa's Grotto alone. It's like I'm actually in the North Pole, working alongside all the elves in the workshop."

"You've watched too many Christmas movies," he said with a laugh.

She leaned toward him, her thin red sweater decorated

with Santa's sleigh stretching across her chest. "But don't you just love them? I could watch them all year round. There's something so feel good about them. You know that they'll end with a happily ever after. You know nothing really terrible is going to happen. And I love anything that has the Christmas spirit. It makes me…" She wrinkled her nose as if she were searching for the word, then just shrugged and said, "Happy."

He nodded and handed her a cup. "I'm surprised I didn't catch you sitting in Santa's chair."

She drew in a deep breath and looked at him in mock horror. "I can't sit in that chair—it's only for Santa. Doing something like that might get me on the naughty list."

"Somehow, I don't think you've ever been on the naughty list."

She nodded. "Oh, I have. A few times. But I'm trying to behave myself."

"Well, don't try too hard." He handed over the bag of cookies. "Now, they might not be yours, but given the time of night, I think they'll do."

He cast his eyes toward the desk. It was covered in translucent colored paper, cardboard, cotton wool, glitter, and glue. Bits of glitter stuck to Lara's cheek and shimmered on her hands and sweater.

He reached over and brushed his thumb against her cheek, wiping some off. "Having fun?" he asked as he showed her his thumb.

She froze, her eyes dilating as she stared at him. His breath caught somewhere in his throat. Tiny dots of glitter still gleamed on her skin. The bright light behind her illuminated her in a way that meant he just couldn't look away. And he didn't want to. He wanted to be right here, right now.

Her voice was a hoarse whisper. "More than I could have imagined," she said.

He reached over, cupping her face in one hand and leaning toward her. She didn't hesitate. Instead, she wrapped her hands around his neck and let their lips meet. The smell of her Christmas spice perfume wrapped around him. Every part of him wanted to pull her toward him, yank her off that chair and onto his lap. The temperature had dropped in Santa's Grotto. Her skin was slightly cold to his touch, but her lips were definitely warm.

He pulled back a little. "Isn't this against the rules?" he said throatily.

She gave a weary laugh. "I can't wait for this to be over," she admitted. "I want to win," she added, "but I also want to see what happens next."

The tiny cradle in his jacket pocket felt as if it were burning. The wastepaper bin beside her overflowed. He had no idea what her tree decoration might be, but he had a horrible feeling it might not be as good as his.

He rested his forehead against hers for a moment. "How about I walk you home? This all ends tomorrow morning.

We really only need to wait until then. We won't be opponents anymore, and we can do whatever we want."

Her eyes were bright. "I like the sound of that."

"So do I," he said as he slipped his hand in her and headed toward the main exit.

He pushed it lightly, but it stayed closed. Frowning, he gripped the handle and tried again. Still nothing.

"Ben?" Lara asked, a frown creasing her brow.

He let go of her hand and pushed his shoulder against the door. It didn't budge.

Lara's hand went to her mouth. "Do you think Ali came and locked up while we were in the back?"

"She didn't come in to check you were gone?"

Lara waved her hand around the room. "I was in here earlier. She probably just looked in here and assumed I'd gone home."

Ben tried to the door again. Then stopped to look at it. "This is an old-fashioned lock and key door. There's no inside latch. We can't open it from here."

Lara's eyes widened. "Of course, they rebuild it every year. It's been around since I was a kid." She spun around. "Are there any other exits? Do you remember?"

He shook his head. "I think this is the only door."

"Oh no." Her voice was quiet.

Ben walked back through to the room at the back. There was a small window covered with a red velvet curtain. He pulled it back, staring out to the street beyond. "There's no one around. Maybe someone will come by later." He tapped the back pocket of his jeans. "Darn it, I left my phone in the workshop."

"Of course…" Her voice brightened, and she fumbled with her bag. "I can call Ali. She'll come back to let us out." A few seconds later, she pulled the phone from her bag, but her face fell. "Oh no, dead as a doornail. I forgot to charge it earlier."

Ben paced around the room, as if a magic door were going to appear out of thin air. "What are we going to do?" He turned toward the tree. The white lights still flickered. "Would Ali normally leave the lights on?"

"They're on a timer," Lara said. Just as the lights flickered for the last time and the place fell into darkness.

"Perfect," Ben groaned.

Lara started to laugh. A deep, throaty laugh that seemed to come from the bottom of her boots.

It was infectious. After a few seconds, Ben started to laugh, too.

"This is ridiculous!" He waved a hand in front of himself, trying to find her in the darkness.

"It's the dream I always had a child," she said, still laughing. "I always wanted to be trapped at Santa's Grotto. I never believed it would actually happen."

Her hand brushed against his. He grabbed it, pulling her toward him. "It's a long time until morning. What are we going to do?"

His eyes were starting to get used to the darkness now. He led her through the dark room, where a tiny bit of light from the streetlights reflected inside.

"I guess we're going to have to find a way to get comfortable," she said simply.

He nodded. "And stay warm."

In the dim light, he could see her smiling. "Well, we have some leftover coffee and cookies, so we won't starve."

"I think we can last till morning," he agreed. He moved over to the back of the room where the sacks for the presents and some large red blankets were piled up. "Want to try these?" He put some down on the floor.

Lara moved over next to him and sat down, pulling the blankets up around her and patting the space next to her. "Might as well get comfortable."

He hesitated for a brief second before sitting next to her. When he put an arm around shoulders, she rested her head against him and sighed.

"Guess it's not how you thought you'd spend the night," he said.

"Only in my best childhood dreams," she replied.

"Are you sorry you took part in the contest?"

She waited a few moments before answering. "No, because I did it for the right reasons. The money would really help the residential home. The other night with the choir? It's the happiest I've seen them all in a while. It's like they finally managed to get a little of their Christmas spirit back.

And that meant so much to see." Her hand rested against his chest, and she looked up toward him. "So, win or lose, it has to have been the right decision, don't you agree?"

Tears brimmed in her eyes and he tensed. He leaned a little closer, his lips brushing against her skin. "So, why are you sad?"

Her voice trembled slightly as she answered. "Because," she paused, "tomorrow, we'll learn who wins and who loses. We can't draw. It's not possible. And if I don't win—and I understand that—I still have to walk into that residential home every day and feel the weight of all their disappointment. I feel guilty for getting their hopes up in the first place. It seemed like such a good idea to begin with. I never actually imagined I'd get to the final. But now that I'm here? Winning has become a possibility to them all. And there's an expectation. Some of the residents don't have anything else to think about. It's become almost an obsession for them. And I created it. Because I took part." She bowed her head slightly. "I think I took part without fully realizing the consequences."

There was silence for a few moments as he contemplated what she'd just said. He understood every single thought, every single emotion, because he felt them, too.

Her hand squeezed the shirt at his chest. "You must feel it, too," she said—as if she could read his thoughts.

He gave a slow nod. "I do. Most of the kids in the high school have a hundred and one other things going on at home—some I know about and some I don't. I always try to be positive around them. I talk to them about failing. About how I didn't make it as a baseball player, and how I had to rethink my life and find myself a new career."

"You do?" She looked surprised.

He nodded. "Of course I do. They're kids. They were born to ask difficult questions. And I'm almost always honest with them."

She gave him a curious glance. "Almost always?"

He nodded again. "Yes. It depends on the kid and where they are at that moment in time. It's instinctual. Some kids aren't ready to hear certain things at their current points in life—even if they ask the questions. I have to put them and their welfare first. It's a judgment call. I tell the truth..." He screwed up his nose, "Ninety-five percent of the time. The rest? I tell a modified version of the truth. I never lie to them."

"Wow," she said softly. "I had no idea how intense things were."

"It's why I entered," he admitted. "Sometimes, I'm their safe place. I never, ever take it for granted or forget it. The gym hall is worn down. If it had a new flooring and better equipment, I'd be able to offer more options for the kids. And you're right. The consequences of this contest have reached further than I ever expected. They've been *so* enthusiastic, so excited. So motivated. For some of them, there's been a spark in their eyes that's been missing for a while.

And even managing their disappointment at the trials we've lost has been tougher than I thought." He gave a thoughtful nod as he looked at Lara again. "I guess we've both learned something here."

Even with only the outside lamp light, he could clearly see her brown eyes. Just one connected look made his skin catch fire. It was just the two of them. They were both clearly affected more deeply than expected by this contest. Tomorrow, one of them would be dealing with the repercussions of losing. It made his heart sink in his chest. He didn't want that. But, somehow, even more, he didn't want that for Lara.

They had this moment right now—this night. It might never happen again. He had to tell her how he felt.

"But with all of this…" He took a deep breath. "I'm still glad that I entered—because if I hadn't, I wouldn't have met you."

Her hand slid behind his back, and the grip on his shirt tightened. "I can't imagine how I hadn't met you before," she said slowly. "We drink in the same coffee house. Live in the same town. Eat in the same restaurants. How come we've never noticed each other?"

He'd had the same thoughts. Over and over. "Life," he said with a resigned tone. "We've both been busy. I was away for a few years, and so were you. In the last few years, you've been busy with your grandmother and I've been busy with the woodshop and the high school kids. We have to take this for what it is."

"And what's that?" she asked.

"Fate," he said decidedly. "We said it before, and we should say it again. Maybe there's a bigger picture. Maybe this contest was just meant to be so we could meet. Maybe someone upstairs has a big plan for us and we're just finding out about it."

"But I want meeting you to be happy time. Tomorrow, one of us will be disappointed. We can't pretend it won't happen."

"Then we have to promise each other."

"Promise each other what?"

"That no matter what the outcome is tomorrow, we won't let it affect us. We won't let it affect what happens next."

"Do you really think we can do that?" Her voice sounded hopeful.

"I think we can insist on it. And I think I know how to seal the agreement." He pulled her closer, and she smiled.

"What did you have in mind?"

"This," he said, connecting his lips with hers.

Chapter Sixteen

HER NECK WAS sore, and she'd lost the feeling in one arm because of the way she was lying. But she was definitely warm—even though the air around her was chilly.

She could hear a noise in the distance. One that she couldn't quite place. And why was her mattress so hard?

"Look at them," someone whispered, not so quietly.

"They've been here all night?"

There was a gasp. "Oh no. I locked them in. I just assumed that Lara had gone home."

At the sound of her name, Lara sat bolt upright, her eyes trying to make sense of where she was.

There was a thin line of early morning sun streaming through the small window.

The blankets tumbled from her, making her conscious of the heat next to her. Ben. She'd been lying in his arms. She'd been in his arms all night long.

Before she even had time to sort out her thoughts, there was a sharp voice from the doorway. "Oh, this is a disaster. Exactly the publicity we *didn't* need."

She frowned. That was Marty's voice. She nudged Ben

with her elbow. "Ben, wake up. We fell asleep, and the…" She scanned the people in the doorway. "Um… staff are back."

Ben made a soft kind of grunt, then his eyes flickered open. He stayed on the ground as he tried to focus. "Lara?" he said with an edge of confusion.

"Wake up," she urged. "We have company."

He rubbed his eyes, then pushed himself up so he was sitting alongside her.

"This is a disaster," Marty snapped, pushing his way into the room and shoving a newspaper toward them. "Your antics have made the whole contest look invalid. Like the whole thing was fixed."

Lara shook her head as she reached out for the newspaper, her stomach already in the pit of her stomach. She'd already been a subject of a scandal once, and she wasn't entirely keen to see what the next episode would be.

The picture was in color, but blurry. It showed the two of them intertwined, Ben's arms around her as she lay sleeping next to him with her arm wrapped all the way around him. It was clear from the odd angle that the picture had been taken from the small window.

This headline was much worse than the first one. *In bed together—the Christmas contestants—has it all been a fix?*

Lara's chin nearly bounced off the floor.

"It's everywhere," Marty ranted. "Look at your phones."

"Do you think if either of us had our phones, we would

have had to spend the night in here?" Ben said with more than a hint of sarcasm. He barely glanced at the paper, merely shaking his head.

But Lara clutched it tightly. "That horrible photographer. How on earth could he do that? He took pictures of us, knowing we were stuck in here, and he didn't help? What kind of a rat fink is he?"

"That kind," Ben said, pointing to the title. "Can I look at your phone?" he asked one of Santa assistants, who still stood in the doorway in stunned silence.

One of them nodded and handed over her phone. Ben quickly searched, then let out a large sigh, turning the screen so Lara could see the page.

The KNWZ publicity stunt.
Christmas couple or Christmas con?
Contestants get too cozy.
Red light needed at Santa's Grotto.

"Oh no." Lara's was sure her face must have paled in horror at that last one. She shook her head, then realized they were still sitting on the floor. The floor where they'd spent the night wrapped in each other's arms. A private moment. That had been shared with the whole world.

Marty was clearly furious. "Of all the stupid, ridiculous, preposterous things to do! This is awful. The phone lines at the station are going crazy. No one believes the contest is for real anymore." He shook his head as he paced about, oblivious to the silent crew filing into the room.

Of course. Filming was due to start in here in—Lara

glanced at her watch—in around an hour. Had they really slept that late? It was nearly eight o'clock. She never slept that late.

Ben had taken off his jacket. After a chilly night in here, it was clear he was feeling the heat in more ways than one.

Marty stopped a few inches from Ben's face, obviously ready to start another rant, and Ben held his hand up directly in front of his face. "Enough!"

The sharp words made every head in the room turn. "Get a hold of yourself, Marty," Ben snapped. "Lara and I have been stuck in here all night. We both want to go home, get cleaned up, and have something to eat. I don't care about your headlines. I don't care about that photograph. Have you any idea how much the temperature falls in here at night when there's no electricity?"

Marty opened his mouth as if he were going to try to speak, but Ben clearly wasn't prepared to listen. "We've taken part in all your tasks. We've done everything to help with your publicity. But enough is enough. Win or lose, you can have one more hour of our time and then we're done."

He shot Lara a glance, not even waiting for her to agree.

"We're adults. We don't need to explain anything to anyone. And I certainly don't feel the urge to explain anything to you."

Lara had picked up his jacket. She held it against her chest as he spoke. Something dug into her. She moved the jacket a little, and an item fell into her hand.

She let out a little gasp. It was beautiful. A tiny wooden crib with a baby inside. The carving was so intricate she could even see strands of straw at the base of the crib. Something clicked in her brain. This was the baby Jesus in his manger.

There was a thin gold strand of string on either side, tied at the top. This was Ben's Christmas tree decoration. And it was one of the most beautiful things she'd ever seen.

She looked up at him. But he hadn't noticed that she'd seen it. He was still arguing with Marty—and Marty didn't look like he'd win that argument anytime soon.

Her hand was trembling, and her mouth felt like someone had just stolen the moisture from it. She glanced at the table, her heart sinking like a stone. They hadn't talked about their decorations.

She'd spent hours trying to dream up something unique and imaginative. But no matter how hard she tried, she just couldn't find something special enough. In the end, she'd grabbed some black cardboard and cut an intricate window frame, filling individual tiny panes with colored film like a stained-glass window. She'd concentrated hard, even trying to do a Christmas design on the window. But when she'd held it up to let the light shine through, it just didn't quite have the effect she'd hoped for.

Now, holding Ben's decoration in her hand, it almost seemed like she could feel all the hopes and dreams of her grandmother's friends slip through her fingers.

Her decoration was almost child-like. She blinked back tears, pushing Ben's cradle back into his pocket.

He was madder than she'd ever seen. And he was letting Marty have it.

"I won't have you blame Lara and me for this. *You* created this mess. *You* wanted the publicity for your station. We're just the bystanders. Us and the kids and the people we've tried to represent. Have you any idea the expectations that have been built? How much this money could mean to them? Or do you not really care about that—is this just about you, and the show?"

Ben shook his head fiercely. "Lara and I are not your fall guys. It's your duty and responsibility to get on air and say, no, we're not fakes, no, we didn't know each other, and it's no big deal we got locked into Santa's Grotto—a place you sent us—and we decided we didn't want to freeze to death last night. Just think about the publicity that would have created for you this morning!"

The anger was starting to leave Marty's face. It was clear he'd only been thinking about himself. And Ben wasn't having it.

He put his hand to his chest. "Have you any idea what these past weeks have been like? I have a whole school full of kids who have staked their hearts and souls on this competition. I'd love to get them a new gym floor, but I'm mostly worried about how they might feel if they see something they enjoy get pumped full of bad publicity. KNWZ has a responsibility to set the record straight."

He didn't even wait for Marty's response. "Ready to get out of here, Lara?"

She nodded quickly. His response had been so impassioned it had touched her heart in a way that told her everything she needed to know.

Competition aside, Ben Winters had captured her heart.

He was dedicated to those kids. He wanted so much to give them better facilities. He wanted to give them something permanent and a safe space.

And she wanted him to give them that, too.

And that was the thing she needed to think about most.

She walked over and joined him as they stepped out into the fresh snow.

"Sorry," he said quietly.

"Don't be."

"Can I walk you home?"

She took a deep breath. "Maybe not. I need a little bit of space." She handed him his jacket and pretended not to see the flash of hurt in his eyes.

"See you at ten?"

He nodded as he slipped on his jacket, his eyes never leaving hers.

"Okay then," she said, forcing herself not to pause as she turned and walked down the street. Her chest felt as if something had clamped around it.

It felt like she had to make a choice—between her grandmother and Ben. What on earth was she supposed to do?

Chapter Seventeen

T HE MOOD HAD changed. It was obvious as soon as he stepped back inside the grotto. Lara wasn't there yet. That much was clear.

Marty was in a corner, talking quietly with someone. All the equipment was set up near the giant Christmas tree—where the two decorations would be hung before being judged by the people here and the listeners online.

His hand folded around the crib. He hadn't said a word, but he'd noticed Lara's stain-glass window. It was cute. It was nice. But he didn't think it would beat his baby in a manger. And he wasn't sure he wanted to do that to Lara.

His heart gave a horrible twist in his chest. The thought of betraying the kids at school went against every principle he'd ever had. His loyalty was to these kids.

But his heart belonged to Lara.

His brain twisted this way and that. Struggling to find a solution—a happily ever after for everyone. But try as he might, it wasn't there.

For the first time in years, he wished he still played professional baseball. If he did, he'd have enough money in his bank account to fund the new floor with barely a blink.

He sighed. Baseball was a lifetime ago. Now, he had the woodshop, and though he hoped things would do well, he didn't have a spare ten thousand dollars right now.

A few of the kids were there, waiting to see what would happen. He made his way over. "Hi, guys," he said. His stomach curled, and he could hardly look at them.

"What's wrong?" Rudy asked.

"Is it because of the photo?" Mari asked. "Because we thought you looked really cute."

He bit his bottom lip for a second. "Guys," he said slowly. "I want you to be prepared that we might not win the competition."

Rudy blinked in surprise. "Of course we will. In it to win it." The words made Ben cringe, because he knew that he'd used them, too.

"Sometimes the important thing is taking part," he said carefully.

Mari's eyes narrowed. "Has something happened?"

Ben shook his head.

But Mari was far too smart for that. "Well, what is it?"

Ben shifted uncomfortably. Nothing like a teenager to put him on the spot. "I just think there's a chance that I might be able to look into other ways to get us funding for the new floor."

Rudy folded his arms across his chest. "Dude, you didn't make anything yesterday, did you?" He gave Ben a cross between a knowing look and a disapproving stare. "All you could see was hearts, right?"

It was like a complete role reversal. Rudy was the coach and Ben was the teenager.

Ben shook his head. He'd always been honest with these guys, and he wanted to keep doing that. "What I'm trying to say is I think I have to do something that might look like the wrong decision, but my gut tells me it's the right decision. I want you all to know that no matter what happens today, I'm here for you all, and I'll find a way to get improvements for the gym floor. For everyone."

Mari folded her arms, too. "You've got it bad, haven't you?"

Ben put his hand on her shoulder, but she shook her head. "Do what you need to do."

He gave a grateful nod. "You do know I love you guys, don't you?"

Rudy waved his hand. "Go. Do what you have to do."

Ben nodded, relief flooding through him. His hand tightened around the wooden carving in his pocket as he made his way through the side room.

SHE SAW HIS pale denim shirt disappearing into the other room as she walked through the door. Part of her had wanted to stay at home and not come back.

But she knew that some of the residents of the home would be here watching, and she just couldn't let them down.

Or could she?

She loved Christmas. She loved everything about it. The colors, the music, the smells, but, for the last hour, it was like moving in shades of grey.

She'd got home, then showered and changed before gulping down a bagel and a cup of coffee. The whole time, her brain had whirred.

It was like being torn down the middle. Part of her was full of Ben. There was no denying it. There was no pretending. Every time she closed her eyes for half a second, she could feel the touch of his lips or remember the smell of his aftershave. Last night was permanently etched on her brain.

But it wasn't just the kiss. It was the connection. His intensity. His passion for his work. His commitment to the kids he coached.

Most people would just assume as an ex-baseball player, Ben would just want to keep his hand in by doing a few hours with the kids. They would have no idea it wasn't just about teaching a kid how to throw a baseball. For Ben, it was about a healthy mind, healthy life. It was confidence. It was inclusion. It was finding the sport or activity that was right for that kid. It was letting them know they could talk and their opinion would be valid. He invested so much time and energy in these kids, and they surely deserved their new gym floor.

She blinked back tears. Some of the radio staff swarmed around her, firing off questions—wanting to do her makeup. She shook her head. "I'm fine the way I am."

She stared at the side room again, wanting to go back in there. Her decoration was on the desk. It wasn't great—and she didn't even want to use it now. She wanted to be clear about her intention. She didn't care what any newspaper said, or what they thought. She wanted the world, or at least the people who listened in Vermont, to know how she felt.

She took a deep breath and made her way over to her grandmother and her friends.

"Lara?" The questioning tone in her grandmother's voice told Lara everything she needed to know.

She wrapped her arm around Edith's neck. "I love you, and I don't want to let you down," she whispered.

Her grandmother took a firm grip on Lara's shoulders, pulling her back so she could look at her face. "Honey, you could never let me down. I'm so proud of you. What on earth is wrong?"

Lara blinked back tears and forced a smile. "I know we won't win."

Her grandmother laughed. "We don't care about winning. We've had more fun in the last two weeks than we've had in months. You did that, Lara. You did that for us. It was never about winning."

Lara's heart swelled in her chest. "Are you sure?"

But her grandmother didn't get a chance to answer before Marty's voice floated across the airwaves. "Welcome to KNWZ."

It was clear he'd managed to pull himself together. It was time for Lara to do the same. Ben stood next to Marty. He stared straight ahead.

Lara moved quickly, ignoring the frantic motions of the radio staff as she ducked into the side room and grabbed some pale blue cardstock and scissors.

She worked speedily, scribbling with a pen and tying some thread before taking her position at one side of the tree.

"Ah, there you are," Marty said pointedly.

She ignored him. Her heart was thudding too quickly in her chest. She couldn't really concentrate. A crowd had gathered all around Santa's Grotto, and the main windows and doors were opened wide.

She tried not to let her fingers grip too tightly to the card in her hand. It wasn't much, anyway. But her nerves could ruin it.

The music started for the show and she took a deep breath, closing her eyes for a second. She had to go with her gut even though parts of her brain screamed at her. That tiny competitive edge she'd always had was making the most noise of all. But she remembered her grandmother's touch. Her words. Nobody understood Lara like Edith did.

The fear and dread she'd had about disappointing her grandmother and her friends had stopped hanging over her like a cloud. She could maybe still try to find a big Christmas tree for them. There had been lots of publicity around this contest. One of the tree lots might even donate one. She could phone around later.

One of the team gave her a nod, and she moved to her side of the tree. It was so big that she couldn't see Ben at all. Maybe this was for the best. Next time they'd see each other, this would all be over. And she couldn't pretend she wasn't glad.

She was ready. One the count of three, they would hang their decorations on either side of the tree. Marty would describe them to the listeners, and the viewers on the live stream would be able to see them.

Ben and his gorgeous crib would win. The kids would be over the moon.

She nodded to herself. This was right. She knew this was right.

Marty chattered in his best presenter voice. "So, after the reports in some media this morning, we wanted to give our contestants a chance to explain themselves."

They did? First she'd heard about it, and a mild wave of panic washed over her.

This wasn't supposed to happen.

But Marty was still talking. Now, she hated the fact she couldn't see Ben. Would he be happy or mad about this? She wasn't exactly sure how she felt explaining herself to the world. Did she really have to do that?

But Marty was around the other side of the tree. She waited while her stomach clenched in knots.

"So, Ben, would you like to give the listeners an idea of what happened last night—and where that photo came from?"

She heard Ben drawing in a deep breath. Could almost see his broad chest expanding and his muscles contracting. He wouldn't be any happier about this than she was.

"Marty, it's like this. As an adult, I don't really need to explain myself to the state. But you set us a task and gave us a place to meet. We followed the instructions of the radio station, which ended up with Lara and me accidentally locked in here last night. It was a cold night, and we had no option but to try to keep each other warm. If we both hadn't been adequately dressed, this could have been a whole different story this morning."

His voice was deadly serious. Ben wasn't making light of this at all. He continued. "As for the photograph, that's interesting, isn't it? You've got to ask yourself why the same photographer that pursued us before knew where to find us. And why he didn't see fit to try to let people know that we were obviously trapped in a place with no heat, no electricity, no food, and no water."

Lara smiled from the safety of the other side of the tree. She could imagine the panic on Marty's face right now. There was a long, uncomfortable silence. Yep, Marty was panicking.

"But there is something else I want to say."

Lara straightened.

"Without this contest, I never would have met Lara. So, even though at times I've had doubts about taking part, she's made it all worthwhile. I love the Christmas season, and sharing this season with Lara has been a joy and a pleasure. I've worked hard with the kids from Briarhill Falls High, and I want them all to know how completely and utterly proud I am of their commitment and dedication."

Marty spoke, his voice a little hesitant. "So, do you have your Christmas decoration for the tree?" He seemed desperate to get things back on track.

There was a pause, then Ben spoke more quietly. "I do."

There was a rustle, and Lara held her breath.

After the longest silence, Marty just said, "Oh."

There was an intake of breath from the crowd at that side of the room. One of the women put her hand to her mouth and let out another little, "Oh." But hers sounded much more affectionate.

Lara's stomach gave an uncomfortable twist. She'd expected them all to be *oohing* and *aahing* over Ben's baby in the manger.

Marty appeared next to her, dressed in his burgundy velvet jacket trimmed with gold. She couldn't read his face at all.

He gave a little twitch as he held the microphone toward her. "So, Lara, do you have your decoration for the tree?"

She nodded and lifted the blue paper heart and looped the gold thread around one of the branches. Written in capital letters, it clearly said—*LET BEN WIN*.

There was a murmur around her, along with knowing smiles. Marty made a strange sound at the back of his throat. "Well, folks," he said quickly, trying to gather his thoughts. "Things have not gone quite as we expected this morning. You may wonder why I haven't described the tree ornaments yet. Let's just say I'm acting on impulse." He leaned forward, taking a small step over, obviously to see Ben.

Then he gave his showbiz smile to the crowd. "What do you say we make them both swap sides?"

The crowd let out an impulsive cheer. Lara was confused. The lump in her throat was currently so big she couldn't even swallow.

Marty gave her a nudge. "Go on then." She took a few steps. Ben walked toward her, a furrow in his brow. It was clear he was just as confused as she was.

The crowd started clapping excitedly, and Lara's curious footsteps picked up pace. She scanned the other side of the tree, looking for the cradle. But it wasn't there. She couldn't spot it anywhere.

Then her eyes fell on something else. A pink paper heart. Her hand was shaking as she reached out to touch it. As she turned it toward herself, she could see words written on the card. LET LARA WIN.

Her hand shot to her mouth, and tears filled her eyes.

Ben had hand-carved that beautiful ornament, but he hadn't used it. He'd done this instead.

It was clear that Marty was as stunned as she was, but true to form, his professional face slid into place.

Ben came around behind her, holding the blue heart in his hand. "Lara?" He was smiling in disbelief. "You did this for me?"

She nodded and plucked the pink heart from the tree as he laughed. "And you did this for me."

He nodded, sliding his hands around her waist. But he didn't get a chance to do anything else before Marty was next to them.

"So, for those at home, it seems that our Christmas love-birds have decided to let each other win the contest. We could never have predicted this, but…"

Lara turned to the side so she could see him.

"The producers at KNWZ have been delighted with the publicity of our Christmas contest. We've decided to turn this into an annual event. But to finish off this year…" he did that big pause again, "We've decided to have two winners!"

The crowd in the room erupted.

Lara and Ben looked at each other, equally stunned.

"What?" they said simultaneously before turning, arms still around each other, to face Marty.

He looked very pleased with himself as he kept talking constantly to the listeners at home.

Lara and Ben didn't get time to do anything else. Ben was deluged by the kids, and Lara ran over to hug her grandmother and the rest of the people from the care home. "We've done it! We can decorate for Christmas!"

She couldn't believe it. She couldn't believe it had actually happened.

But it didn't take Ben long to find her again. He slid his arms around her waist, pulling her toward him.

"I saw it," she whispered. "The beautiful baby in a manger—why on earth didn't you use it?"

"Because you were more important," he said simply. "I knew how much you wanted to win for your grandmother, and I thought I could try to find another way to fund the gym floor for the kids." His face broke into a wide smile. "But I guess I don't need to now." He shook his head. "What about you? You were about to give up your dreams for me?"

She put her hands on his shoulders. "Like you, I thought I could try to phone around the Christmas tree lots and stores, see if I could get some to donate on the back of the contest. I thought I might not need to win the money. And you—you were so committed to the kids. I didn't want them to be let down."

His hand slid through her hair. "Lara Cottridge, you're a good person with a huge heart."

She looked down for a second. "Yeah, there's a problem with that."

"What?" Ben's fingers tightened at her waist.

Her eyes gleamed as her arms moved from his shoulders to around his neck. She stood up on her tiptoes. "It seems that someone might have stolen it. Someone named Ben Winters."

His grin spread from ear to ear as he bent toward her. "Merry Christmas," he whispered.

"Merry Christmas," she whispered back as she ignored everyone else in the room and kissed the man she loved.

The End

If you enjoyed this book, please leave a review at your favorite online retailer! Even if it's just a sentence or two it makes all the difference.

Thanks for reading *The Christmas Contest* by Scarlet Wilson!

Discover your next romance at TulePublishing.com.

TULE
PUBLISHING

More books by Scarlet Wilson

The Christmas Brides series

Book 1: *The Runaway Christmas Bride*

Book 2: *The Jingle Bell Bride*

Available now at your favorite online retailer!

If you enjoyed *The Christmas Contest*, you'll love these other Tule Christmas books!

Royally Abandoned
by Sarah Fischer & Kelsey McKnight

A Christmas Romance
by Nancy Holland

Boyfriends of Christmas Past
by Edie Grace

Available now at your favorite online retailer!

About the Author

Scarlet Wilson wrote her first story aged 8 and has never stopped. She's worked in the health service for over 20 years, training as a nurse and a health visitor, and now currently works within public health. Writing romances is a dream come true for Scarlet and she's published with Harlequin Mills and Boon, Tule Publishing and Entangled Publishing. Scarlet lives on the West Coast of Scotland with her fiancé and their two sons.

She loves to hear from readers and can be reached via her website www.scarlet-wilson.com.

Thank you for reading

The Christmas Contest

If you enjoyed this book, you can find more from all our great authors at TulePublishing.com, or from your favorite online retailer.

TULE
PUBLISHING

Made in the USA
Middletown, DE
28 October 2020

22896489R00137